Edge of the Desert

Edge of the Desert

GIFF CHESHIRE

Sagebrush
Large Print Westerns

Library of Congress Cataloging in Publication Data

Cheshire, Gifford Paul, 1905-
    Edge of the desert / Giff Cheshire.
        p.   cm.
    ISBN 1-57490-054-4 (alk. paper)
    1. Large type books. I. Title.
[PS3553.H38E33   1997]
813'.54--dc21   96-53966
                                                                        CIP

Cataloguing in Publication Data is available from
the British Library and the National Library of Australia.

Sagebrush Large Print Westerns are published in the United States
and Canada by Thomas T. Beeler, Publisher, Box 659, Hampton
Falls, New Hampshire 03844-0659. ISBN 1-57490-054-4

Published in the United Kingdom, Eire, and the Republic of South
Africa by Isis Publishing Ltd, 7 Centremead, Osney Mead, Oxford
OX2 0ES England. ISBN 0-7531-5527-3

Published in Australia and New Zealand by Australian Large Print
Audio & Video Pty Ltd, 17 Mohr Street, Tullamarine, Victoria, 3043,
Australia. ISBN 1-86340-685-9

Manufactured in the United States of America

CHAPTER 1

JIM CARLIN WAS IN THE PASS, MOUNTING TO THE moccasin table, when the crash of a rifle split the late-day silence, and his horse whirled as if stung by the bullet, then began to pitch. He felt the surprise go through him like a breathed anesthetic as he yanked up the animal's head. He swung the mount hard around and saw a spurt of bullet-thrown dust on the spot it had just vacated.

His first thought was that, somewhere beyond the pass, a branding fire burned illegally, with a slick-ear due to be tabbed. He swore for he had no gun with him. By then he had managed the worried horse into the rocks and the shooting stopped. Jim's shock wore off, the horse grew calmer. Looking down, he saw a welt across its withers, the hair clipped and burned. In a moment hoofs jarred Nebraska's parched earth, fading fast into the pass.

Jim Carlin was a reckless man, but not so foolish as to ride unarmed into an unknown situation. Easing the horse on through the rocks, which threw the heat of the day they still carried, he came back to the trail at a point lower in the pass. On the bench, when he came out, he received another surprise.

Bolder stock thieves would shoot at a man to hold him back while they destroyed evidence, if possible, and got away. Nowhere in the open twilight distance could he see the smoke of such a fire, there were no fleeing riders and no cattle or horses in sight to tempt some passing renegade. In his excitement he had jumped to the obvious and wrong conclusion. The shots had been

1

aimed at the horse, not him, trying to drop it. If he had been set afoot he would have blamed it on some thief not meaning to be caught with the goods. He would also have been stranded out here too long to make the water meeting in Moccasin. The lines of his mouth pulled flat and long, and he rode on.

He never liked coming into Moccasin, at least not in the past year, for it had a stricken look. He felt its impact, like that aroused by beloved dead, whenever he glanced along its single street and saw the empty eyes of so many deserted buildings. A railroad had killed the cowtown, bypassing it and building, ten miles away, the drab, dull farm town of Prairie City.

He saw Al Vassey and Harry Sands at the foot of the lodge hall stairs, slack-stanced and silent. The horses racked there and in front of the saloon across told him the cow country was out in force to stand for its right to Silver Lake, now a pitifully small contingent of ranchers.

"Hoped you'd be here, Jim," Vassey said, for Jim had no lake frontage, no voice in what tonight would be decided. Ranching south of the main cattle community, he was not in close touch, although this meeting had been called ten days ago by a man now dead. Boyd Peyton, who had ruled the country, had been willing to temporize with the land-grabbing settlers. It remained to be seen whether his son and heir was of the same disposition; on the son depended the fate of the lake country.

"Somebody didn't want me here, though," Jim answered. "Tried to shoot the horse from under me in the pass."

"No fooling?" Vassey said sharply.

A solid man, he was still young, with the neck of a

2

bull and a jaw to match. He had inherited Roman Five from his father, who had been one of the first to run cattle around Silver Lake, and his roots went deep. Silver and its fringe of range-dotting lesser lakes was the last stronghold of the range industry in the Panhandle. Custer County was lost, the Platte Valley was surrendered, the entire area southeast of Moccasin and northeast around Prairie had been taken over. The settlers pushed, they never relented, never considered what they were doing to other interests and older inhabitants. Vassey's temper was dangerously on balance, ready to let go at any excuse.

Harry Sands shifted the thin length of his body. His brand was the Lazy S on the Red Butte, north of Silver and above Vassey's Roman Five. He looked drawn, discouraged. "Why you, Jim?" he asked. "Your spread isn't on the lake. Anyway, the deal's cut and dried. Crown holds the high hand on this range, while the rest of us have never drawn the right cards. We'll do what young Peyton decides, and if he didn't intend to go ahead with the deal he'd have called off this meeting."

Jim let a scowl build on his brown face, a lithe, rangy man whose shaggy hair was black and whose cool eyes were precisely the same color. He said, "I told that promoter Gallant his whole Prairie setup was a swindle and nothing else even if old Boyd never suspected it and young Peyt still don't. It could be Gallant doesn't want me to explain why I think so at the meeting."

"Except on general suspicions," Vassey said, "why do you think so? The sodbusters back him right down the line."

"General suspicions are enough. A specific one is that no honest man needs to keep a bodyguard around like that gunhawk of his. That's who I think laid for me this

3

evening."

"We'd better get upstairs," Vassey said. "Somebody's started talking, and it sounds like Gallant."

The three climbed the steps to the second floor of what had been the town's biggest store until the homesteaders put an end to so many cattle ranches and the railroad delivered the coup de grace. Lanterns had been lighted against the evening darkness of the big old hall. The heat of the space carried the smell of ancient dust and ancient times, and the present emptiness reminded Jim keenly of the day when every bench and chair would have been occupied at a meeting as deadly serious as this one.

Now half a dozen men sat around a table in front of the room, where the light of hanging lanterns brought out the hard intentness of their features. At the head of the table, silent while the newcomers found seats, stood Gallant, the man who had built Prairie City and was now developing an irrigation tract in the country surrounding it, complete with everything except the water needed to attract buyers. Jim noticed at once that Lagg, the gunman, was not present. That was strange, for Gallant never entered the cattle country without him. To have sacrificed that protection, he had thought it important to keep his one open accuser away.

On the promoter's right sat Peyt Peyton from Crown, the boss outfit of the lake country, newly placed in control of the key ranch by the sudden death of his father just a week back. He was as tall as Jim but more solidly built, his crisp dark eyes and hair made him sleekly attractive, and he had a relaxed detachment his father had never possessed. He tipped a nod to the newcomers, the only one besides Gallant who seemed aware of their arrival in the in-turned tension in which

4

the rest sat.

"I was telling the others," Gallant said then, "that it's as important to me as to you to settle this water question peacefully. You know I want a right-of-way through Crown for a ditch to carry water to my tract. The project's been approved officially and the land optioned to me, contingent only on work being started to carry water to it."

"Us little fellows were called here to be forced," Vassey said angrily. "There's no need to beat around the bush. Boyd Peyton was for your having your ditch. Peyt must be or we wouldn't be here listening to your song and dance."

Peyt Peyton flung Vassey a narrow look that was curiously unruffled considering the lifetime enmity between the two. In a voice so mild it surprised Jim, he said, "Boyd called the meeting, Al, not me."

Gallant straightened his shoulders as he glanced at Peyt, seeming bewildered himself by the man's good humor. He was tall, with a body of hard-knit flesh, and there was nothing in his worn sack suit and rumpled shirt to suggest the money he was investing in Prairie. Yet, Jim reflected, there was much in his shrewd gray eyes to indicate how he got it.

"If you want tough talk, Vassey," Gallant said, his voice roughening, "I can make it, too. Let's start with the facts. There's four cattle outfits tying up Silver Lake, which holds many times the water they need. There are three more on the inflow streams, one on the overflow creek. Eight of you holding water you don't need that would provide farms for hundreds of families."

"That's not the whole story," said Harry Sands. "Get a boom started here, and more settlers will come in than

5

you can handle. They'll run over us like a herd of buffalo."

Jim nodded, and as he did so saw Gallant fling Peyt a look that indicated he expected backing he wasn't getting so far. The promoter let eyes that were now angry and aggressive play over the others.

"Did you men ever hear of eminent domain?" he asked. "Make me go into court and I'll cut not only your water but your range to what you've got legal rights to. If you hired a hundred lawyers, they couldn't stop it. You don't think I'd spend the money I have if I wasn't sure of that, do you?"

"We knew what Boyd's attitude was, Peyt," said Burt Tantro from the Cutbank. "But you haven't made yours clear. What is it? You own the only land Gallant could flow water across."

"It's the same as Boyd's was," Peyt answered. "He saw a lawyer who told him Gallant can do just what he threatened—get water and a lot more than he'd be willing to settle for to save himself time and expense. But the right-of-way isn't everything. Three of you own rights on the lake. I could sell the ground but you could get an injunction against the ditch and tie it up in court just as long. So you've got as much say as I have, and I went ahead with this meeting to give you a chance to say it."

"You're letting us have a free choice?" Vassey asked disbelievingly.

Peyt looked surprised. "Why shouldn't I?"

Jim had a feeling that Peyt wasn't behaving the way either Gallant or the ranchers who expected to be bossed around had anticipated. The promoter watched the young rancher thoughtfully. More moderate than before, he said, "Men, face the facts. You can't stop homesteaders from following a railroad into a new country. You can't keep me from getting them water. So I've got a simple compromse. Help me settle them on my farm land, and I'll do all I can to keep them off your range, where they'll go looking for watered land otherwise."

Rye Jones, whose Fishhook lay on the west end of the lake, shook his head stubbornly. White-haired and craggy, he had trailed longhorns from Texas and was completely intolerant of the changing times.

He said, "You can't come to terms with a sodbuster under any arrangement, Gallant. We tried it in Custer County, me, Charlie Vassey and Bill Trevers. That was all cow country then, and Kearney was just a cowtown. Herds from Texas used to ship there as far east as Schuyler. Look at it now—farm country from one end to the other."

Bill Trevers, a lake-fronter with Jones, Vassey, and Peyton, had his headquarters on the south side at the mouth of the Dry. He was a tall, lank man, as old as Rye and just as bonded to the past.

"We had a place to move to get away from 'em then, Rye," he said uneasily. "Now we don't. There's no more range to be had."

He subsided into uncomfortable silence for his position was painful. Memories, not only of the old trouble in Custer County, but of all the years of ranging and working cattle around Silver, made him feel keenly what Al and Rye felt. On the other hand, Peyt was going to marry Bill's daughter after the fall roundup and apparently still favored the proposal. Bill found himself hauled back and forth across the fence.

Bitterly Al Vassey said, "My dad, you, and Bill fought it out down there, Rye. Boyd Peyton quit—run for it. Come here and grabbed off the best range while

7

the rest of you were so hard hit you never could recover. And all because you three were men enough to stand and fight."

The detachment vanished from Peyt's face. The flats of his hands hit the table as he came to his feet. "I told you once, Al," he breathed, "that if you ever called my father a coward again I'd kill you."

"Have at it!" Vassey cried, springing up. "A Peyton'll do the slick, slimy thing every trip. This time there's no place to run, so you think you can buy off the nesters with water. The only reason you're not acting eager is you think Gallant's threat to take range and water both will force us into line. Then you won't have to make threats. Your future wife wouldn't like that, since she happens to be a fine girl."

The pressures in every man there stood boldly to the surface in the sudden clap of quiet. A muscular tic marked Gallant's cheek as he saw the end of his hope for a quick solution. The older men, Trevers and Jones, sat strained and intent, struck dumb by the moment's impact. The three ranchers from the more outlying regions showed a gleaming-eyed support of Vassey. Had Vassey and Peyton worn guns, they would have reached for them. Now they stood ready to tear each other apart, out of their old hatred as well as this instant.

Knowing he had kept out of it long enough, Jim Carlin rapped out. "Simmer down, you two. It's not what Peyt might be trying to do, Al, it's what I know damned well Gallant is trying for. He can't afford to go to law or let you take him there. His threat to take water and range both is pure bluff—he can't do it."

"Now just a minute," Gallant cried.

Jim stared him down. "You can't wait, Gallant, you've spent too much money without getting much

8

back from it yet. You can't even get full control of the desert land you hope to sell without the assurance of water. So my advice to the others is to stand pat and check the bet to you."

"Naturally I've made a big investment," Gallant said furiously. "On the assurance of competent lawyers that I've got a legal right to Silver water."

"Did you mention to your lawyers that your only aim is to peddle as much desert land as you can call watered then clear out and let it go broke? In which case we'd have ten times as many settlers swarming over us, like Burt said a while ago, as we'd have if we don't help you bring in the suckers."

"That's ridiculous."

"So you told me the other day. If so, why did you send your gunman to try and keep me from repeating what I said to you here?"

"I don't even know what you're talking about," Gallant returned.

"Then come downstairs and see the bullet burn on my horse. The rest of you, too. I warned you I'd point out the bugs in your joy juice, and your gunhawk tried to drop it in the pass tonight."

"That's a bald-faced lie."

"If Jim says it happened, that's enough for me," Rye Jones said, climbing to his feet.

"Damn it, Peyton," Gallant said urgently, "you've got to make these men listen to reason."

"It looks like you're going to have to prove your good faith," Peyt said, and actually smiled at him.

Vassey rose to follow Rye Jones out, then all but Peyt and Gallant were moving toward the door.

Jim showed the others the bullet mark on his horse, although proof of what he had charged upstairs was not needed by then. The others rode out of Moccasin, taking the lake road, but since Jim's outfit lay six miles south of Silver, on Dry Creek, he again cut across country, traveling alone.

Here on the table, the land was so open the emerging stars swung down to the horizon. The eternal breeze of the high plains fanned him, carrying the scents of the edging desert that for nearly a generation cattlemen had looked upon as a sterile buffer, protecting them from what they had suffered elsewhere. Then a railroad had broken down that barrier, an event in the name of progress that had worked on cattleman nerves ever since. This night, although the meeting had broken up, had built the tension to the intolerable point in Gallant as well.

Jim's own edgy watchfulness as he rode made him more than once swing to take a long, careful look along his back trail. He rode fast, doubted that anyone could have got ahead of him, but even so as he reached the ridge where he had been shot at he paused to listen a long while before he risked riding through.

When he was over the ridge he could see down into the sink he had wrested from the wastes and made his own, land nobody else had wanted. Long ago, when the water flow had been more vigorous, the Silver's runoff—enormous in the rainy season and barely a trickle in the dry months—had backed up here. Now it had shrunk so that, even in the most violent storms, the bed of the creek carried it off into the southward wastes. The dry sink had been a mixture of sour marshes and arid worthlessness until he homesteaded and drained it. An equally great labor had gone into the catch basins he had built farther down the water course on the public domain. As a result he owned the best wild hayland in the vicinity, could range cattle south into country previously useless but now as attractive to entrymen as the rest of the country.

Gallant would now have to make it an open fight. As long as he appeared honest he had the more favorable legal ground under him. He had the backing of the Prairie business people, eager for a land boom, and of the settlers already located and those arriving with every train. Even if he wanted he could not relent, having boomed the project through advertising and by word of mouth until it had an impetus that would roll over even him if he failed to make good his promises.

Jim puzzled over Peyt's actions that night, which had had the same effect on everyone there. His father had favored trying to localize the settlers and avoiding the legal expense trying to deny them what, if it went to law, they were bound to get. Peyt had disclosed a like leaning, yet had done nothing to use Crown's power in support of Gallant, which Boyd would surely have done. Vassey had mentioned Peyt's future wife and probably had come close to the mark. Nora Trevers would never stand for the highhanded tactics old Boyd had sometimes used on the little outfits, of which her father's was one, and people who had been her lifelong friends.

Jim reached the little sodhouse where he had lived alone for five years, hoping that this loneliness would in time be relieved, and he had known from his first days in the lake country who he wanted there with him. But she had already chosen Peyt, although the wedding had not been scheduled until recently. Jim feared for her without knowing why except that Peyt Peyton was too much an unknown quantity for him to feel otherwise.

CHAPTER 2

FOR A MOMENT AFTER THEY FOUND THEMSELVES alone in the Moccasin hall, Peyt stared at Gallant with a lingering amusement that was even a little reckless. "What're you going to do now?" he said, and his voice conveyed a taunt.

Gallant took a cigar from his pocket, fastened it in his teeth, then forgot to light it. A restless desperation deepened the lines of his angry face. In a bitter voice he said, "Your father told me, before I spent a cent on Prairie, that he approved and would help me get water without a lot of legal delay. He could have. Why couldn't you?"

"I told you Boyd's old rough stuff is out, Gallant," Peyt said easily. "And I told you why."

"Is your girl against the ditch? Her father was on the fence, at least, till Carlin shot off his mouth."

"She's for whatever I am," Peyt answered, "except for Crown cracking the whip the way it used to. She's made that plain."

"What am I to do?" Gallant said, throwing up his hands. "Carlin was right about my not having time to go to the law. God, man, you don't realize the expenses I have, the pressure on me from the people around there. I thought I was ruined when I heard your father had died, then I saw you and you said you saw it the way he did."

"I also told you I don't have the power he had, at least not the same kind."

"Maybe you like seeing me over a barrel."

"Do I?" Peyt said cheerfully, and he walked out.

When he reached Prairie City, Gallant drove to the livery barn, where a hostler stepped from the shadows.

12

"Evening, Mr. Gallant," he said unctuously to the town's founder and leading citizen. "Have a nice ride?"

Gallant didn't answer the question as he swung out of the rubber-tired buggy. On the ground, he asked his own. "Have you seen Honey Lagg this evening?"

"At his hotel, probably. He put up his horse a while ago. He was in a bad humor."

"Tell him I want to see him."

Gallant strode along the town's new boardwalks to the Granger, a solid hotel of two stories, square and high above the false fronts running along either side of the new railroad tracks. He had rooms on the main floor, and as soon as he entered them he went to the center table in the outer room and poured a stiff drink. His nerves were badly shaken for in Moccasin, for the first time in his experience, he had found himself caught in the kind of trap it was his business to set for others. Peyt Peyton was playing a two-sided game, there was no doubt about it. He had gone ahead with the meeting as he had promised, then sat back to let things take their predictable course.

Gallant took a swallow of whisky then, carrying the glass, hung his hat on the deer antlers on the wall. There was a mirror framed beneath the mounted horns, and for a moment he stood looking at his image, aware of the tic in his cheek that always betrayed his tension. What he saw otherwise was as impersonal to him as the desert land he meant to turn into a fortune. He knew that he presented a forcible if middle-aged appearance, possessing no handsomeness. That lack had never troubled him. The plundering of men was more satisfying to him than the conquest of women, and he had a disturbing intuition that he had fallen into a like power possessed by another.

13

Honey Lagg lived in a cheaper hotel down the tracks, but was not long in answering the summons. He was—which surprised Gallant each time he remembered how ruinous the man could be—of slight, almost wispy stature. Most men removed their hats when they came into Gallant's quarters, but Lagg never did. He only pushed the dirty Stetson to the back of his head, tipping a wary nod.

"Pour yourself a drink," Gallant said.

Lagg did, but before he tasted it he looked up dubiously. "I don't like the politeness, Gallant. You're going to give me hell for missing Carlin's horse."

"I told you to keep him away from Moccasin," Gallant snapped. "And he almost beat me there. I supposed you were as good a shot as you claim."

"It was getting too dark," Lagg said anxiously. "Anyhow, from the way that horse acted I pinked it at least. Before I could do more, Carlin swung it into the rocks. I was scared to keep after him once his wind was up. You know what they say about him. In a tight spot he's a real cougar."

"I thought you're supposed to be."

Lagg looked injured. "You said not to do anything that could be traced to you. What if he'd plugged me? Everybody knows I work for you, and after he got into the rocks he had the edge."

"It's going to be a tougher fight than I wanted," Gallant said. "They turned down the deal because of him. So they've got to be forced into it, and I don't want another upset from him. The next time try your luck on him and not his horse."

"That," Lagg said, "calls for more money than you pay me."

"Do it so I don't get blamed, and you'll be paid what it's worth."

14

Lagg's vanity rose on his face. "A Pinkerton man tried to figure out who killed a fellow I know about," he said. "He couldn't do it. When do you want it done?"

"The first good chance you get—with the light right." Gallent smiled thinly. "Tell me something, Honey. With a nature like yours, where did you get that name?"

"A whore gave it to me and it stuck."

"You keep bad company."

"Couldn't help myself. She was my mother."

Bill Trevers rode with the main group of lake ranchers along the old Moccasin trail, which curved around the west end of Silver and came back on the north shore to Roman Five, the Lazy S, and Fred Downey's outfit on upper Red Butte Creek. Bill was deeply troubled by what had happened in town. Not only had he seen a veiled, simmering proof in Gallant of what Jim had charged about his dishonesty. Peyt's actions had puzzled him, conveying to Bill the impression that Peyt hadn't cared one way or another how the thing turned out, whatever his father had favored.

It was too bad Gallant's proposal could not be trusted for it left the farmer problem as pressing as before. More than once, coming out from town, Bill had caught himself watching forward trees and rocks, carried back years to the old days and the trouble then, when a man could have used two pairs of eyes. He had learned several lessons back there, where he had been forced to detect danger almost by its smell. Here in Nebraska the homesteaders had been the ones to organize, made arrogant by their great numerical superiority, and they had been guilty of everything ever charged by their kind to a cattleman.

Just trying to live next door to them was impossible. They squatted everywhere, plowed under good grass,

fenced water holes and cattle trails with a state law—
passed by granger politicians—protecting them. They
came in droves and always won. Some made a success
of farming the dry country, most didn't, and wherever
they showed up they put a quick end to the cattle
business except for the small barnyard variety that Bill
despised.

His companions had pulled inside themselves also,
but when they reached the turnoff to Tack, Bill's spread,
they stopped there for a last exchange of talk, as they
always did.

Turning to Vassey, who started a cigarette, Bill said,
"How's your mother, Al?"

"Not good," Al said, tapping tobacco into a paper.
"Doc Winthrop says she'll have to get to a warmer
climate next winter, but I don't see how I can raise the
money. Guess I will somehow."

Bill nodded. Ellen Vassey and his own wife, Lucy,
now dead, had been close friends. It had grieved him
when rheumatism turned Ellen into a helpless cripple
almost as much as if it had been Lucy. Al had already
been put to a heavy medical expense, and like the other
small ranches around the lake, Roman Five had never
been much more than a meal ticket.

"That's something I'm thankful for," Rye Jones
reflected. "Me and Martha have had wrinkles in our
bellies sometimes but we've been healthy. People are
lucky to reach old age that way, and we know it.
Anything Martha can do to help, Al? You know how
she likes to."

"No, thanks," Al said. "We get along."

They were all dodging the thing Bill knew to be
uppermost in their minds, and all at once Harry Sands
said, "Damn it, boys, if a bird was to sneeze in one of

16

them bushes I'd hit for cover. Walking out on Gallant was the only thing you three could do, but I don't like what I see coming."

Nobody answered. Depressed, Bill said good night and turned up the long, straight lane to the low-roofed house that stood against a bluff of the Dry, close to its mouth. There was a light in the window, and it was early enough that Nora might still be up. He let out the little yell he always gave to let her know who was arriving. When he came into the house after turning his horse into the big pasture, she was sewing in the lamplight.

Looking up, she smiled a greeting, a slender, dark girl who in her fresh prettiness reminded him so strongly of her mother at about that age. Although he had grown too old to think often of such matters, he knew she had Lucy's warmth of nature, too, her capacity for loving the man of her choice with all she had. He was secretly unhappy that she had promised that to Peyt, although it had seemed likely since the two were children together.

"Did they get it settled?" she asked.

Bill shook his head and was silent as he hung up his hat and found his rocking chair. He filled his pipe and lighted it. "The meeting broke up. Too many signs of a bear trap in Gallant's proposition, and Jim Carlin pointed them out."

Nora looked up with the tension so weighting the lake people since the settlers began arriving nakedly traced on her young face. It was harder on the women, maybe, without a man's tough fiber to help them. Any peaceful solution seemed worth trying, and he knew she had shared Boyd's belief that he had found one, a belief Peyt also seemed to hold although he had done nothing to force it through.

17

"How could it be a trap?" she asked.

"Jim accused Gallant, the other day, of being another slick land promoter, interested in this country for what he can take out in a suitcase. If he brings in hundreds of settlers, sells them land, then runs out on them, they'll be stranded on that desert down there. What's worse, they'll crawl over us trying to find land they can live on."

"Maybe so," Nora said. "But what makes you think Jim's right about Gallant meaning to do that?"

"I told you he accused Gallant before. Then somebody tried to shoot the horse from under him to keep him from repeating it at the meeting where Gallant made a mighty reasonable plea for a settlement."

"You're all keyed up," Nora said hotly, "and it's made you imagine things. Jim could have spread his suspicions any time. So why was it necessary for Gallant to keep him away from Moccasin tonight?"

Bill looked at her narrowly. "Jim's not the kind to make talk against anybody unless he's got good reason. He had to hear what Gallant was going to say before he knew he had reason."

Uncertainly she said, "What does Peyt think about that?"

"I just don't know," Bill admitted. "He had me puzzled. He talked like he thought Gallant's ditch would do what he claims the last time he was over here. But tonight he didn't seem to give a hang if it went through or didn't. The only time he showed feeling was when Al reminded him his dad run out on the rest of us in Custer County. In fact, Al implied that Boyd had been getting fixed to do it a second time, and they nearly tangled."

"Well, I don't blame Peyt for that. He's heard about Custer County all his life. Al never missed a chance to mention it, and neither did Wade and Emery Jones when they were alive. Their fathers were let down, they'd say, while Peyt's sneaked away from the war and got all the best range in this country in return for it. It's envy, that's all, and Peyt has a right to resent it."

"Just the same," Bill said, himself growing testy, "when the grangers organized against us down there Boyd took his herd and slipped away without telling us. It left a big hole in our defense and we were cut to pieces. We got here broke, and he was all set to rule the roost. According to him, he did us a favor even letting us in on the lake—the parts, by the way, he didn't need himself. He always let us know who threw the long shadow, and I always thought it was guilt on his part that made him like to do it."

"Maybe he did," Nora said, and her jaw set as she completed a stitch. "But Peyt doesn't intend to be that way. We've talked about it. If he didn't press for what he wanted himself, it's because of that, and a lot of gratitude you're showing."

"We might as well face it," Bill returned. "Others beside Al think there was a secret understanding between Boyd and Gallant. Another underhanded move to save Crown no matter what happens to the rest of us."

"If Peyt didn't press for it," she cried, "how can they think he means to do the same thing?"

"Mainly," Bill said, getting to his feet, "it's the idea that a Peyton's a Peyton. Now hold on. I didn't say I subscribe to that." He put his pipe on the mantel, feeling weak and old and tired, and went to bed.

As he rode out for Crown on the lake road, well behind the others, Peyt was well satisfied with the way the meeting had turned out. He could even dismiss the

19

dig Al Vassey had made about Boyd. He rode swiftly, recklessly through the night, feeling its coolness and the contentment that had been in him ever since he got control of Crown, to which Nora soon would move to live with him. The road ran northwest so as to curve around the end of Silver, and when be reached the Crown turnoff he took it without slowing his speed. On the last rise before Crown he looked down through the starshine upon the spread's sprawling headquarters.

There were a dozen men in the bunkhouse down there who now called him boss. They were rough, hard, experienced punchers—Boyd had always picked that kind to protect him and his interests, to insure his control over the lake country. But there was one Peyt meant to replace, Guy Gordon, the ramrod, who had never liked him or bothered to conceal the fact. He would do that next. He would then have the situation and the crew he wanted, and there would be exciting work to do.

As he passed the lake road that ran from Crown to Tack he thought again of Nora and the marriage that now was so near. All through the years she had been the only person in the lake country he liked, who took him for what he was instead of Boyd's son—the offspring of a coward and traitor—and his need for her was desperate. Except for her and his terror at the thought of losing her, he would not have worked through Gallant, as he now had to do. He would have relished making the lake country feel the naked power of the new Crown, of its new master, watching them revise their opinions of a Peyton's weakness. He reached headquarters, put up his horse and went to bed in the empty old house.

He awoke the next morning to hear the wrangler bringing in the day band, and from a window of the big house, presently, watched the men in twos and threes come out of the mess shack and go down to the corral to rope out their forenoon mounts. This morning he had the feeling, while he watched the familiar action, of the riders running Crown under the direction of Guy Gordon, who in turn was motivated by a momentum picked up under Boyd. That was another reason why Guy had to go; not only did he resent and resist Crown's new head, he was too thoroughly saturated with Boyd's thinking and methods.

When he saw the foreman come out of the mess house, using a toothpick, Peyt slid to the door, stepped out, and walked briskly over to him.

"Morning, Guy," he said pleasantly as they came together.

"Morning," Guy answered. He sounded impatient.

Leathery and burly, he wore the fiercest mustache in the Panhandle. He had worked for Boyd nearly as long as Peyt could remember and had but one interest— Crown and its cattle. He could run the work as well as Boyd, and even this morning he showed Boyd's impatience with the man who was now his boss. His breakfast eaten, Guy wanted to do the next logical thing—get busy without interference in the routine he knew better than the man who had stopped him.

Crown range swept north past the railroad, east almost to Prairie, then wrapped around the southeastern edge of the lake until it joined Tack, sending a wing along the north side to Roman Five. In the old days, when the lake outfits held free sway, all the cattle had run more or less together and at will, as far as the Running Water and south to the Platte. But for years, as sections in the outland fell to the plow, this had shrunk, until now a more careful management was required.

21

After spring roundup Crown had in recent years moved its cattle into the choppy hills girting the railroad to the east and let them run there handily until the beef gather. With settlers now moving into the hills, this required much riding on the part of the punchers. Also, during the summer months, there was wood to cut on the pine buttes and haul in, there were horses to break for fall roundup and the railroad drive, wagons to get ready—a hundred things. Guy had his schedule worked out precisely and never deviated if he could help.

With this in mind, Peyt said, "Guy, I've decided to move the spring gather up north again."

For a moment Guy stared at him. "What on earth for?" he said at last.

"There's still enough grass there to carry them through to fall, and it's risky running them so close to the nesters around Prairie."

"But," Guy protested, "that'd make the beef gather twice the work, and it would double the drive afterward."

"This year we'll ship over the new railroad."

Guy looked stunned. All through the years Crown beef had trailed south to the Union Pacific. He pulled up his thick shoulders, and his eyes bulged as he stared.

"Why in hell," he demanded, "didn't you say so after the calf roundup, when it would be easy? Now we'll have to round 'em all over, and I'm too busy."

"Do you recognize an order, Guy?" Peyt asked softly.

Guy's dull stare broke into a sudden bright anger. Peyt met the surge of the man's will calmly, his eyes never wavering.

"All right," Guy said. "Write it out."

"Write what out?"

22

"My check. You never had grounds to fire me, so you've tried to make me quit since the day of your daddy's funeral. It worked, and I hate to think of what's going to happen to Crown with you running it. To the rest of the country, for that matter."

If Peyt had any hidden regrets at getting rid of this old employee, they vanished at that. He swung on his heel and walked to the ranch office, where he wrote out the check that paid Guy off. As he blotted it he was thinking of the man who would be his new foreman, promoted over the heads of a number of older hands but man enough to make it stick, Tex Rinehart, who was as good with his gun as with his fists. It didn't matter right now whether Tex had Guy's knowledge of cattle.

CHAPTER 3

JIM CARLIN AWOKE WITH A HEAVY SENSE OF oppression and knew there was something more pressing than routine work to be attended to immediately. In his sleep, long in coming because of a restlessness left by the meeting in Moccasin, his deeper mind had taken over, sorting the many questions and shaping some kind of general answer that seemed trying to burst into his awareness. A man of considerable intuition, he was used to this feeling, a little like birth pangs, that meant an idea was coming. All at once, when he stepped outdoors to wash up in the light of the morning star, it came through, and he wondered if there was a scheme afoot involving more than water from Silver, perhaps more than Gallant and the settlers he represented.

He wrangled the horse pasture on old Pedro, whose habit was to hang about the flat-topped soddy at night, and on the claybank he had that spring bought from Al Vassey he rode north after breakfast across the old dry lake bed toward the narrows. There beveled bluffs pinched in to a width of a quarter mile, and the narrows were divided by the Dry, which now meandered, slow and sluggish, down the center of the sandy channel.

An impatience gnawed him at this distraction when work was heaviest, and beneath that was a continuing tightness of nerves at the threat he so strongly felt. As he rode he thought of what he had at stake, of the five years he had put in building a cattle spread out of the leavings of the others. Around the first of April he had turned out his dry stock, following in two weeks with the cows and calves. When the general roundup worked his range in June, he had branded over a hundred calves. He had, afterward, few animals to be brought to the bottom for special handling. He knew that in October he would again have premium beef to load out for Omaha at Pine Bluff.

His was the only herd around Silver that wintered in, and during the warmer months he could graze his cattle well south into Nebraska's butte and rock country, for the thin pasturage there did not have to carry them all year. He irrigated only the wild native grass on his hay bottom and did not mow it, letting it cure in the dry hot air so that the cattle themselves could crop it as needed. If he had the water there were hundreds of acres more he could put to such use, but only so much came down the moody little Dry in the rainless months when water was so important.

No man in the Panhandle pounded more leather than he did, for he liked to cover the range as often as possible to determine the location and condition of the scattered stock, check on the grass and water holes, and make sure no strays had taken off for far places,

24

voluntarily or driven by some rustling outfit ventured down from the mountains. There were sometimes wolves, also from the higher ranges, and bogged steers or a cow come upon trouble in calving. There would now and then be a dogie to bring in to the hospital bunch, and always on his mind since the railroad was finished was a cowman's deepest dread—settlers showing up on his water.

A half dozen homesteaders dotting his range in the wrong places could render the whole useless to him. He had three natural waters out there, plus half a dozen handmade ponds along the winter course of the Dry that filled anew each year. Each of them was a powerful attraction to the land-hungry hopefuls who thought they could dry-farm that part of the table. Every other outfit in the lake region was equally and in a like manner exposed to them. Yet the suspicions now turning in his mind, keeping the edge on his nerves, were more definite, more focused than this.

As he rode north toward the lake Jim made first for the foot of the yellow bluffs breaking up to the Moccasin table for easier riding. Due to this unexpected change in direction, he saw a horseman swing his mount hurriedly into the concealing rock at the base of the low cliffs. Jim pulled up the claybank in quick uneasiness, pondered briefly, then rode on. When he looked back a little later no one was visible, yet his tension remained.

He reached the edge of the fallen rocks and followed along until he came upon a place where, in some bygone drought, somebody had tried to tap a vein of table water by digging a well at the bottom of the bluff. Riding up to the dry hole, he dismounted, threw the reins over the horse's head, and dropped them so they hung into the well, their ends out of sight. He moved quickly thereafter

25

into the sandstone cluttering the base of the rim. He wore a gun now as a result of the previous night's experience.

Al Vassey had trained the horse well, for it stood patiently. In about five minutes the curious picture it made, there above the hole with the reins dangling in, produced the effect Jim wanted. Honey Lagg was on foot as he prowled forward to investigate, and at first Jim saw only the peak of a worn, high-crowned hat. The fellow came within twenty feet of where he crouched, then stopped to take a long, wondering look at the horse.

After a moment Lagg stepped forward, keeping wide of the horse, wary as an animal yet drawn on. He came up to the edge of the hole, stared down in deepened bewilderment, then because there was nothing to be seen down there he swung and threw a worried, betrayed look about him.

"Did you think I had a mine down there, Lagg?" Jim said.

Honey Lagg's hand made a reflexive move toward his gun but he controlled and stopped it when he saw how close Jim's hand was to the grips of his own. Jim stood by a big rock, and Lagg was close enough to see the black whirlwinds in his eyes.

"Well, I never seen a horse tied to hole in the ground before," Lagg said, and tried to laugh.

"You're out early this morning, and missing no bets. Gallant must be pretty sore about you missing a good one in the pass last night."

Lagg jerked up his shoulders, and all at once his eyes were ugly and unamused. "You're all they say, ain't you—a real ringtail?"

"If you make another try for me, Lagg, you won't live long enough to find out. I had to be sure it was you, and the next time I'll kill you on sight."

26

Lagg's little eyes were lively with the vain urge to take over the play. But the black eyes he watched showed him a cold, lethal light. For a long breath he hung there, then the kill-readiness left him. He turned his back in an effort at disdain. Jim watched until he vanished into the far cover, then mounted the claybank and rode on north.

When he reached the woody shore of Silver at the mouth of the Dry he halted to sit his saddle and smoke a cigarette. The lake was a mile wide, three long, and nobody knew for sure how deep. There was a million dollars' worth of water out there if Gallant or anybody else could put it on the market, while many times that amount wasted down the Dry each winter. Now he stood face to face with one of the things that had burst into his mind that morning, forcing him to take a look at the lake at once.

Here at the mouth of the drainage creek the low bluffs pinched in even more. A man who wanted to invest the money to throw a simple earth dam from one wall to the other could double the amount of storage during the dry months, and the sloped shores would allow it without drowning any important property. Not only would that provide much extra water. It would give enough surface elevation at the proposed take-out point on Crown to let the whole Prairie desert be irrigated. Maybe he had been wrong about the fly-by-night nature of Gallant's undertaking, for the desert was much larger than the tract at present laid out around Prairie City. But the error would be only in the length of time Gallant meant to operate—Jim was still positive that once Gallant had milked the project for all he could get he wouldn't care what happened to it or the country around it.

Jim's horse showed interest in something behind and, remembering Lagg, he swung it hastily and was relieved

27

to see Bill Trevers ride out from the low, hugging shoulders at the Dry gap. Jim eased off and waited for the old man to come up.

"Seen you go by," Bill said. "What're you doing up here so early? Usually you're on the range before I've got off my straw tick."

"I'm scared, Bill," Jim said, pointing at the gap. "If you built a dike across there you could put me out of business. You might find yourself set to put some other spreads out of it, too."

"Did you get pitched off on your head?" Bill asked. "Such a thing never occurred to me."

"It might have occurred to somebody else." Jim went on to explain what he had just wondered about.

"True enough," Bill said, "but it happens I own that gap. It's on my patented land."

"Men have got hold of property they want before, Bill."

"Gallant will play hell getting hold of Tack."

"His gunman's still after me. On my trail again this morning. I tricked him into my own hands and warned him that the next time I'll simply kill him."

Bill's seamy face showed shock. "What's he after you for now? You did your damage last night."

"Maybe I started more than I stopped."

"It's a cinch Gallant's got too many blue chips in the game to pull out." Bill pondered a moment, then shrugged. "Mind doing me a favor? I forgot to tell Nora I'm going up to Fishhook to see Rye. Stop in and tell her I won't be back for dinner, will you?"

"Sure," Jim said, seeing through it at once. Bill always threw him with Nora when he could, betraying his hope that she would become interested in some man other than Peyt, although it was getting too late for that.

"See you later," Bill said, and rode on west.

Nora was busy with her morning work and apparently thought it was her father who had ridden into the yard and swung down at the edge of the back porch. Then she came to the door, a slim, straight-backed, lovely girl whose fresh neatness and vivid coloring never failed to strike up in Jim a baffled yearning and unrestrained admiration. He saw at a glance that she was annoyed with him.

"Morning, Nora," he said. "I seen Bill and he'd forgot to tell you he won't be back for dinner. He's going up to Fishhook." Knowing she saw through it, which only deepened her annoyance, he grinned at her.

She said, "Thanks," tartly, then good manners overcame her stiffness and she added, "He never gives up, does he?" and laughed.

"Maybe I should follow suit."

At once the wariness he so often saw in her when they were alone entered her eyes. She said, "Don't try to blarney me, Jim."

"You know it isn't that, Nora, and if you were fair to yourself you'd admit you're afraid to trade a lifelong affection for what might prove a new, real love."

"Why, Jim Carlin," she said, and brought down a foot.

"Is that a bad thing to say to an engaged girl? I don't think so. That's what Bill's afraid of, why he does this. He knows how I feel. We'd both make you look around a little, if we could."

"I'm going to be married," she cried, "and I won't listen to talk like that."

"I know you won't. Forget it." He rode on.

Nora did not at once turn back into the house, instead remaining in the doorway and watching Jim's shape grow smaller as he rode down the lane to the road. It

29

infuriated her that so many of the lake people thought her love for Peyt immature, almost a matter of lifelong habit, lacking something they considered necessary. She was thinking now of Martha Jones, Rye's wife, and a comment she made the last time Nora rode over to Fishhook, carrying sewing that invited talk about the coming wedding. Martha was as old and worn as Rye, yet neither of them seemed to have lost the zest for the simple life they had had on Silver, not even after a prairie fire some years before trapped and destroyed the two sons they had worshiped.

"I don't know about you and Peyt," Martha said that day. "If a woman don't turn warm when her man looks at her, it won't work out. I don't think you feel that for Peyt. It's not that you're as used to him as I am to Rye, either. I still get more of a thrill out of that old fellow than I think you get from the man you've picked. Honey, is there something in other men you're afraid of?"

"Of course not," Nora said, aware even then that she had not convinced the old woman.

Just the same, ever since that day, there had been a nagging guilt in her that the only man who had ever made her feel what Martha described was the man now just a spot in the heat-hazed distance. She had felt it just now, his eyes on her with all his feeling showing, a compelling urge to let herself respond to him regardless of the pledge she had made to Peyt so long ago, out of his great need for her even then, that when they were grown she would marry him.

No one understood her deep, sometimes heavy feeling of responsibility to Peyt. Without her it was hard to say where he would be now. It was terrible for a boy to be ostracized for something his father did, whether or not Boyd had been cowardly and treacherous. More than once she had talked Peyt out of a black, reckless mood that had frightened her. As frequently she had lifted him up from the deepest despair. Yet between these extremes there were long periods in which he was gay, spirited, fun to be with, exciting to her even if there wasn't anything very earthy in it. Once they were married she would be a good, full wife to him, feeling everything she should feel.

He would do much for Crown, he hinted at many new plans for innovations and improvements Boyd had always rejected in his rutted ways. If Peyt was a little immature it was because his father had never let him have any real responsibility or independence of action. When Peyt had proved his competence in his own right, as she was sure he would, the lake country would recover from its feeling that Crown was only the fruit of his father's unmanliness and Peyt only the parent's image.

Eased of the guilt Jim had aroused in her, Nora returned to her housework. She knew her father had decided to visit Fishhook only after encountering Jim, but she expected him to do it now and was surprised when, an hour later, he rode in. Hurrying outdoors, she saw that he carried a calf across the saddle and she understood why he had turned back.

She knew at once that the little creature had lost its mother in being born. Unless they got it to nurse from a pan immediately it would never make a good beef. She helped Bill coax it with fingers dipped in a pan of canned milk, and when finally the dogie got the idea and began to suck Bill's fingers she matched her parent's smile. Presently the calf was drinking out of the pan, saving itself from runthood.

31

"So you want some dinner after all," she said accusingly to her father, but made happy again by the calf.

"No hurry," Bill said. He looked embarrassed, knowing she had seen through his stratagem.

She smiled to let him know she forgave him and hurried into the house to start the midday meal. She wished that he at least could be happy with her plans. More and more she realized how important to her it was to have his approval, to be what he wanted her to be, to do what he wanted her to do. All her life she had remembered the deep love that existed between her parents before her mother died—so long ago now—her father's loneliness afterward, and the way he had poured an affection upon her she would not have had otherwise.

She needed affection just as Peyt needed it since they both had grown up motherless, and all at once she wondered if Peyt, since Boyd only repulsed his love, had not turned to her for what she got from Bill when when they were very small, if her breast was not now as important to him as the part by which man and wife were supposed to be united, if her feeling for him was not mainly through the same channel. The guilt returned, her cheeks reddened, and she forced the matter from her mind.

Honey Lagg had crossed the Moccasin road, under a hot noon sun, when he saw Jim Carlin, a roll behind his saddle, cut the road farther down and turn toward the town, apparently without noticing him. Lagg rode out of the butte shadows, into which he had pressed out of habit when sighting a rider, but for a moment reined in the horse again, deliberating. He had meant to visit Moccasin for a drink, but all at once he wondered if it might not be smart to keep out of sight and see where

Carlin was heading that he would need a camp and rifle.

He could see all sides of Moccasin from this viewpoint so, swinging back into the shade, he dismounted and rolled a cigarette. That morning when Carlin had looked at him with those blackly shining eyes, so full of death, Lagg had conceived a healthy respect and an unholy hatred. He suspected that Carlin was going down to the south prairie, where he had cattle, and that was lonely country. He watched Carlin dismount at the Texas hitchrail and go into the saloon.

He had smoked the cigarette before the man came out, mounted, and headed on the other way. Lagg waited a few minutes more, then, swinging into the saddle, rode down into the town himself. He bought cheese and crackers, which he stuffed into his saddle pockets, bought a drink in the Texas, and afterwards he himself traveled south.

He stalked Jim Carlin through the rest of a hot, dusty day, mostly following his trail and never getting close enough to be seen. Step by step he dogged Carlin through his range work as they got down into the rougher country. The man stopped at a couple of ponds to see if they were holding up and whether there might be a steer to be pulled out of the bog. Once he found evidence that led to a tag of strays he threw back, and again there was sign where wolves had pulled down a calf, and Carlin stopped to put out a poison bait.

Honey Lagg had the patience of an Indian on a job like this, and he had an Indian's stealthy quietness and quick, brutal savagery. He had provisions, slim as they were, to stay out as long as Carlin did and he was in no rush for that moment when the unpredictable man might again surprise him. He kept himself out of sight, simply following and waiting.

Toward dusk Carlin reached Kettle Springs and made camp. Lagg had himself stopped there, coming up from the Union Pacific, and he envied the man his ability to drink of the spring's cool water. But all he could do at present was work spit in his mouth and swing down in a ground hollow well away from Carlin's camp.

This looked like the place. There were precious few campsites on the table, and all manner of men used them. Many of them, Lagg knew, came down from the mountains or up from the southern prairies, either riding fast or leisurely prospecting for profits along the way. Some would kill a man for a good horse and saddle or the money he might have on him or a few steers that could be sold to some shady butcher or farmer farther east. If anything happened to Carlin down here it could be made to look like a renegade had done it.

Lagg unsaddled his tired horse, took the bit from its mouth, and hobbled it to let it graze. He knew it was as thirsty as he was, but that would have to wait until later in the night. He ate some cheese and a few crackers, and afterwards tried to pacify his parched mouth with a cigarette. He was about a quarter of a mile from the springs and could relax.

Night ran across the prairie, and he had always liked the time when the first stars burst out. He could remember when as a boy he would sit like this and watch them emerge, one dazzling point of light after another, clear across the sky. He would dream his dreams, and he recalled how they had always revolved about himself as a man seven feet tall with a blazing gun in either hand. He hadn't got much over five feet and could handle only one gun at a time. But he was just as good, otherwise, as that ideal he had seen so often so clearly.

Lagg found himself growing drowsy so finally he sat up, stretched, and yawned. He had picked a place downwind from the springs but even so didn't want to take his horse any closer. Rising, he stretched again, working his thin shoulders to loosen them. He pulled his gun, broke it, and checked the loads. Then he began to move up out of the hollow, very slowly and very quietly.

He had crept in close to the campfire by the springs when he discerned all at once that there were two horses on picket. He halted, puzzled and staring, his eyes raking around the campfire. There were two men there, although one must be lying down for he could see but one seated figure. Carlin had either met someone here by arrangement or a passer-by had ridden in from the blind side and been invited to make camp.

Lagg cursed under his breath, the eagerness he had built up swelling against the frustration. He wasn't going to tackle two of them, for Carlin alone was a handful. He saw his golden opportunity swept from him, then the patience of which he was so capable came up to help him again.

He waited there a long time, and after a while the other man got up and went out to a horse. Lagg had a moment's hope that he was riding off, but the man went back to the fire. Lagg saw the two bedding down and knew he was in for another day down here, with only a saddle blanket and a few more crackers and some cheese. But thirst was his worst prospect, for now he could not get to the spring until Carlin and the stranger had left.

Lagg had an uncomfortable night in the hollow, for the saddle blanket was scant cover. He rose before dawn, stiff and chilled, and saddled up, not wanting to

35

be so close after daylight blazed across the prairie. He kept to the hollow, riding for about half an hour.

He waited until the sun was two hours up before starting toward the spring. Topping the rise, he saw that the camp had been broken and nobody was there. He went on in, flung himself down, and drank thirstily, then watered the horse. Afterward he ate what was left of his rations, looking about. He had long since memorized the tracks of Carlin's horse, and they headed west. The other man had gone east. That encouraged Lagg. Again he took up the trail.

Around noon Carlin came to Pool Table Rock, drank at its spring, then stopped in its thrown shade to rest. Out in the brutal heat, Lagg had to swing his horse hastily into a dry wash that had no shade at all. Hunkered there, he smoked, hungry, thirsty, and tired. But his determination was undiminished. Carlin would be turning back toward home pretty soon. Lagg knew he might have to take a bigger chance than he had counted on.

This might be the place to try his luck. Carlin had shown no sign of suspicion, was not watching his back trail. A while ago they had passed some of the man's Circle C's, and the first thing was to make sure of Carlin. Then Lagg could run one of the steers up here, shoot and halfway skin it. The coyotes would carrion off the flesh, but the split hide would suggest that Carlin had come upon some rough customer trying to have a meal off him and got himself shot.

Lagg put his horse along the wash, heading north. He allowed himself about five minutes, then came up out of the depression, finding that he had got in behind the long flat rock. There was an even chance that Carlin would have concluded his rest and ridden on, but Lagg's blood was coursing hotly as he rode in to the blind side of the rock, dismounted, and ground-haltered the animal. It was easy getting up on the flat top.

The rock was hot, and Lagg slid himself painfully across the surface. He held his breath as he pulled up to the other rim and looked down at Carlin's tempting back. He knew that wouldn't do; Carlin had to face the man who killed him for it to look right, but even then he had no chance. He was seated, and that meant a broiling wait until he rose of his own accord so he would turn his body and not just his head when Lagg called out. Lagg had his gun in his sweating hand and he prepared himself.

Looking below again, he made a sickening discovery. Out at the edge of the shadow, where it lined sharply across the sandy earth, was printed plainly and distinctly the shadow of his own hat peak, which moved as he did. Cursing his own stupidity, he lay with held breath. Had Carlin seen it? Was that nerveless man sitting there planning his own move? Lagg fought down a surging urge to shoot him while he could. He dared not do it. If Carlin had stumbled upon a cattle thief he would have been shot from in front.

Lagg got hold of himself when Carlin still did not stir. He was afraid to try to pull back for fear the movement on that shadow edge would draw notice not yet attracted. Once the man shifted his shoulders, and Lagg's heart raced, but Carlin only pulled out his tobacco. Lagg waited, thinking the crash of his heart must carry down for Carlin to hear, while the smoke was rolled. When Carlin had struck and cupped a match, he bent his head to light the cigarette and Lagg jerked back.

He was weak, his whole body greasy with sweat. He had seized his chance to withdraw that tattletale shadow

37

and only now wondered if Carlin had rolled the smoke to tempt him to do it. Now Lagg was afraid to look over the rim again, even without his hat, aware that a bullet might tear up through the hot air and snap the thread of his life.

Sweat oozed from Lagg as he lay on the blistering rock and tried to think. It dawned on him that he had best get down from there before Carlin treed him, keeping him so until the heat finished him. He began to move back toward the other side of the rock, having trouble being slow and quiet. It took all the nerve he could muster to look over that side even. But nothing happened. He dropped down to the talus and made his way quietly to level ground.

He was aware that he might only have buffaloed himself, yet he could no longer trust the hope that Carlin was not onto him. He was tempted to return to his horse and give it up, but pride would not let him run from Carlin after that humiliation at the old well on Dry Creek. He moved to his right, his gun still in hand, his hat again pulled onto his head.

There was no dispute when he turned the first corner around the rock's west end. That encouraged him to try the last corner, moving an inch at a time. Rid of the momentary panic, he thought there was every chance that Carlin would still be sitting there, unaware of the activity the act of lighting a cigarette had stimulated. From this angle Lagg could fire instantly and without warning.

The rock at his ear gave off a shrill ping before he heard a gun's crash jar through the heat. Lagg whipped backward, almost dropping his gun, the awareness exploding that Carlin had caught onto him beyond doubt. Lagg's knees nearly unlatched when he remembered how far he was from his horse. If Carlin thought of it and set him afoot, he would die off here without food and he had no way to carry water.

The fear was an agony to his pride, and in a moment the pride regained him. Carlin's gun cracked out again, but Lagg could neither see nor hear the impact of the bullet. It dawned on him that Carlin could not know where he was, was shooting at both ends of the rock to hold him back, perhaps while he got onto his horse and away. Sure of himself again, Lagg laughed silently, back at his own game.

His conviction grew when once more rock loosened on the corner ahead of him while a gun's roar split the heat. Lagg dashed forward even as Carlin would be turning the other way. But Carlin wasn't turning. He faced Lagg, disdaining to drop him as he emerged, waiting, his brown face expressionless. As Lagg shot he knew he had been fooled again. Then something smashed into him, and as he fell dying he still saw Carlin, who all at once was the one who looked seven feet tall.

CHAPTER 4

PRAIRIE CITY WAS INDOLENT FROM HEAT AND DUST AND the aftermath of the day's one excitement when the westbound halted to switch three more emigrant cars onto the crowded siding. About the town wheeled a sterile, broiling flat, criss-crossed with new roads and pegged into symmetrical divisions by white survey stakes. Along the wide main street a dozen business houses, moved not long ago from Moccasin, shared with later arrivals such trade as the settlers brought in from

39

the back country, where they were already established on some little sand-hill lake or stream. It was a paltry commerce in proportion to Prairie's ambitions, and now many an investor besides Rodney Gallant was angrily impatient for the water the stubborn cattlemen had refused to relinquish at the meeting in Moccasin the other night.

Standing under the Granger Hotel's long board awning, Sam Weems, the land locator, spoke testily to Gallant as both of them looked down the tracks.

"That makes," said Weems, nodding at the emigrant cars, "six new families with no place to settle till you open your tract. There's nothing left out yonder any more."

"You think I don't know that?" Gallant said.

Ever since the water meeting he had been catching it from all sides. Storekeepers were interested in the booming business promised by Prairie's ultimate development, the new bank as yet was barely able to justify its existence, the hotels were operating at little or no profit. Even more loudly complaining were the new settlers arriving each day, some riding the palace cars as first-class passengers, others with families and belongings jammed into boxcars that rattled in at the hind ends of the daily trains. They all had been promised much more than they were finding in Prairie. Even Weems, Gallant's one intimate, was getting hostile.

"Look, Rod," Weems said, lowering his voice because of the passers-by, "I've been thinking."

His business was simply a service he offered for a fee, that of being intimately acquainted with the surrounding country for miles out, knowing where desirable land claims could be found and helping with the legal requirements. He was smooth and persuasive with the homesteaders, and Gallant had long since agreed to let him sell tract sites on commission, the only prospect left for Weems with the back country saturated.

"So have I," Gallant replied, "but thinking isn't much help right now, Sam."

"That depends on a man's nerve," Weems retorted. Plump and curly-haired, he was the expected in men of his kind, akin to grocery and whisky drummers, or lightning rod and sewing machine salesmen, although a notch or so below Gallant in the fine art of gulling. "There's a way you can put 'em on the tract, build up the pressure on those cowmen, and also strengthen your hand."

"How's that?"

"Go ahead and file your lawsuit, even if you don't want to wait for it to be settled. Everyone knows the government backs these wet-farm projects, that you're bound to win the suit. So you can sell options, with the balance to be paid when the water comes. The settlers will go for it. I've talked to 'em and I know. They'll move onto their places, get wells dug and houses built and their own ditches in. That's all they could do till next spring anyhow. They don't see any reason to be hung up like this. Neither do I."

Interest kindled in Gallant's worried eyes. "You say you've sounded them out?"

Weems took a cigar stub from his mouth and spat across the sidewalk. "As a matter of fact, one man even asked me why he couldn't do that. I felt out some more. They don't want to go off into empty country if they can get a watered place near town. The women like that, it makes schooling the young ones easier, more company, better all around. The ones interested have the money to buy, build, and carry themselves through the winter, which they figure on having to do anyhow. You could have 'em put the money in escrow, to be yours when the ditch is started."

"It's worth thinking about," Gallant said, excited but not willing to commit himself until he had thought it out for his trade had taught him to distrust another man's ideas.

"I wouldn't put it off," Weems warned as he walked away.

Gallant's office was over the bank, and he was thoughtful as he returned there, passing his two clerks in the outer room and going on into his own. Crossing to the window, he looked out at Prairie City, his creation, feeling as he sometimes did that it was not really there but only a mirage raised up on the hot prairie. There was some basis for the illusion, for so far it was mainly a would-be town. The honeyonkers, as the cattlemen called the settlers, sometimes respected the realities. Rarely did a true town boomer such as those who had been drawn here by the railroad and their own soaring ambitions. But realities always asserted themselves, and already an explosive pressure was building up in Prairie.

Gallant was pretty sure Weems had come up with the thing he needed to offset the shocking reverses he had met with at Moccasin the other night. In Omaha a contractor was waiting for word to move in with the men and machinery to dig the ditches that were to run down either side of the railroad for some ten miles. He might well work out a deal with the homesteaders, who would arrive in increasing numbers until fall. With the money put in escrow, he would be as well off as if he collected it on sale, taking the whole into his possession when the ditch work began. He would be able to take full advantage of the mounting demand for land, which would be gone for another year if the ditch was delayed very long.

Gallant had taken steps to overcome the setback at Moccasin, having the day thereafter sent a telegram to a man he knew, saying he wanted half a dozen tough fighters, handpicked and dependable. They were due any time now; he had gone down to the depot expecting them in on the train.

When somebody burst into his private office without waiting to be announced by one of the clerks, Gallant saw not Lagg but Peyt Peyton. Gallant stared at him in surprise.

"I thought you'd steer clear of me now that I've got to get dirty," he said.

Peyt smiled at him. "Nobody from the cow country's going to visit you and find me here."

Gallant was uneasy, for he had not figured out what lay in the mind of this sleek, confident man. He said, "Sit down," and took his own chair at the desk, watching Peyt settle into the one across. He pushed over a box of cigars, but Peyt shook his head. "How about a drink, then?" Gallant asked, and Peyt nodded. Opening a desk drawer, Gallant got out a bottle and a couple of shot glasses.

"Have you got any homesteaders," Peyt asked, "with nerve enough to settle near Silver?"

Gallant gave him a startled look. "I expected some men today who can pass as homesteaders if necessary. What makes you interested in that?"

Peyt ignored both his drink and the question while he pulled out tobacco and started a cigarette. Gallant lighted a cigar while he waited, studying the young cattleman, seeing there a combination of Weems and

43

himself and something much deeper, a riding, deadly purpose.

"Considering what you've been doing," Peyt said when his cigarette was lighted, "you're probably familiar with irrigation laws."

"I ought to be."

"The big stuff. But do you know anything about the old desert act? It was for the benefit of the little fellows and it's still a law."

"The act of '77?" Gallant said. "It's never applied to me."

"It does now," Peyt said coolly. "A man can get 640 acres of this country under that law if he can show he can irrigate it. He don't even have to live on it. If he's got it watered within two years he can get a patent for a dollar and a quarter an acre. That's how Carlin got his sink land."

"Where's there any more like that, and what good is it to me?"

"There's a place," Peyt said easily, "on Red Butte Creek."

"On Roman Five?" Gallant gasped.

"That's right. Above my friend Vassey's patented land. If you had a good man claim it, with a few other good men working for him getting the land ready to water, it might be worth a lot to you."

"And what's it worth to you?" Gallant asked narrowly.

"Never mind my part. For yours, it might make Vassey change his mind about signing a water agreement with you. Rye Jones, too, since he could be treated the same way."

"That's not what you're after," Gallant retorted. "I don't buy pigs in pokes, Peyton. That's the second

44

suggestion I've had today from another man. I've spent too many years coaxing others to play my game to switch roles."

"You want water, don't you? I think you said you'd be broke if you didn't get a ditch started. All right, do what you expected Crown to do for you. Force them to agree, doing the dirty work yourself instead of hanging it on me. You've got to clear out when you've cleaned up, I've got to live here."

Gallant picked up his drink, noticing that his hands trembled. "You've given me a good idea," he said. "I intended to spot some real rough settlers around Silver, but I never thought of that desert claim business. I can even put the squeeze on you. Easy to show how a lot of Crown's open range could be watered from the lake."

"Don't try it, Gallant. I've got a good crew. They can wreck anything I tell 'em to."

Gallant saw his defeat in those smiling, unyielding eyes. "Then show me where the open land on Red Butte is," he said.

Peyt was marking a land map Gallant got out when the door burst open again. Again Gallant saw it wasn't Honey Lagg who arrived. Jim Carlin stepped through, closed the door, and for a moment leaned on the panel. Gallant stared at him, his gaze dropping to see the smashed, dirty hat under Carlin's arm, the extra shell belt and gun in his hand. He knew already that something had gone very wrong, and he felt the muscles of his throat pull tight. Carlin flung a puzzled look at Peyton, who only stared back at him.

Walking forward, Carlin dropped the hat and firearm on the desk. "Recognize these?" he asked Gallant.

Gallant did, but he managed to look indifferent. "Why should I?" he asked.

"That's twice you sent Lagg after me," Carlin said. "And the last time. I buried him down at Pool Table Rock. I've notified the sheriff. He might be around to ask some questions, Gallant."

"Of me? Why? I haven't seen Lagg for a week." Gallant's voice was unsteady for he was aware of his danger, of those killing lights in Carlin's black eyes and the other gun on his hip. There was yet another in Gallant's desk drawer that he yearned to reach for but he knew he dared not try it.

Carlin swung his gaze to Peyt, saying, "So Boyd Peyton's still with us in all his stinking glory. Trying to sell the rest of us down the river."

Gallant saw the exploding fury that had swept over Peyt when, the other night, Vassey had made the same kind of remark. Peyt surged to his feet. Carlin only stood there, almost amused by the shaking intensity of Peyt's reaction. Peyt wanted to draw his gun, he stood there aching to do it.

Gallant had the feeling that Carlin would drive the man into trying, then would kill him, and that would put an end to a ditch across Crown very soon. He made his own bold play then, silently opening the desk drawer and bringing out his gun.

"Carlin," he warned, "let him alone."

Carlin swung a glance at him. His own heavier six-shooter loomed large in its holster; for an awful moment Gallant thought he would draw it.

"Don't be a damned fool, Carlin," Gallant warned. "You came in here and talked rough. Don't make me shoot you."

"Keep out of this," Peyt rapped. "I can handle my own affairs."

"Not in my office. Get out of here, Carlin. If you've had trouble with Lagg, I don't know a thing about it."

46

Carlin pulled in a long breath, looking from one man to the other. Then he swung and walked out.

"Where's that smart head of yours?" Gallant said to Peyt. "Didn't you hear him say he'd notified the sheriff about Lagg? I'm going to have some sticky questions to answer. I don't want any rough stuff added to it."

Peyt was getting hold of himself. "What are you going to say about it?"

"I fired Lagg a week ago, and my clerks will vouch for it. If he had a grudge against Carlin, it was over something I don't know a thing about. If you're wondering why I wanted him out of the way, he's as smart as we are and apt to put some rough going in that smooth plan we were discussing when he walked in. And remember this. After what's happened it wouldn't be smart for anybody to waylay him again very soon."

"What makes you say that?"

"Vassey made the same kind of remark to you, and I notice he's at the top of your list."

Peyt stared at him, then walked out in the brisk way of Carlin.

Gallant put away the gun, rose, and walked to the window, a feeling of unbearable oppression settling upon him. Perhaps it was his age, he thought, the middle years, when contention was no longer a stimulation but a slow wear on the nerves. He was still a gambler, that was part of his nature but all at once he wondered why he had taken a comfortable capital and thrown it all into the game again. Habit, possibly, the practiced routine of cleaning up on one venture and immediately seeking a new one. He drew a cigar from his pocket, snipped off its end with the cutter on his watch chain, then rolled the cigar between his fingers. Then he used his flint-and-naptha lighter to get the smoke going.

He had been worried about Peyton, now he was worried about the sheriff, and he was more acutely aware of the imponderables in what he had to accept, the feeling of being crowded into action by other men for the first time in his life. When could a man begin to feel he had achieved something? All at once Gallant knew why he always had an illusion of unreality when he looked out at Prairie and the simmering desert surrounding it. Actually he had never made a permanent achievement, and now the time of life was upon him when such things began to count.

CHAPTER 5

AL VASSEY HAD BEEN ANNOYED WHEN MOCCASIN'S apothecary joined the rush to Prairie for he was constantly going there after medicine for his mother, not only that prescribed by Dr. Winthrop, who had moved to Prairie, too—but also for one patent medicine and then another in his great desire to find something to relieve her constant, worsening handicap and pain. Now he was riding east across Crown, heading for the railroad town, a bottle in his pocket that had to be refilled.

He was wondering how he would get away on the beef gather, which would start in another month, and whether this year there would be money left after he paid his bills to send her someplace where it would be easier for her to winter. For several years he had broken horses, in addition to his regular work, but even with that income he would have to get a good price for his beef this year and the market so far was not promising.

As he got nearer Prairie, where the land grew flatter, he thought of Gallant and the smooth way the man had

48

cleared himself after Lagg, the ambitious gunman, had tried to kill Jim Carlin. No one in the cow country, probably not even the sheriff, had doubted that Gallant had ordered Jim killed, but that could not be proved and now it was water over the dam. Al had not seen Jim since then; like everyone else, Jim was getting ready for roundup, the single yearly payday of the cattlemen.

As he rode into Prairie's flat drabness, Al noticed at once the emigrant cars strung out on the long siding—that, instead of loading pens, marked a farm town—and he observed that out on Gallant's desert tract several tents had sprung up. As he passed down the string of boxcars he saw children at play in the weeds along the track, he saw limp, grayed washings hanging on improvised lines, and now and then some man or woman would stare at him dully. He felt a quick, hot anger against the people who enticed them to this country—the railroad was as guilty as the land and town promoters—knowing the odds were greatly against their success here, a place to which most of them were driven by adversity and from which they would be driven by an adversity greater still.

Al reached the drugstore and went in, meaning to get his business in this town over as soon as possible. He was out in five minutes, he swung up again and rode west.

An hour later, and only because he turned somewhat north of his regular trail to investigate a buzzard bait that proved to be a dead Crown steer, he came upon wagon tracks. They puzzled him for they were fresh and there was no reason he could think of for the Crown trouble wagon to be up here, where at present there was no important ranch activity. He followed the tracks out of simple curiosity until, later, they left Crown range and entered his own. By then he was growing disturbed.

49

The range on across to the Red Butte was rolling, broken here and there by a low butte or an upthrust of rock. The day was by then far enough along that heat waves shimmered across the land, softening and even dissolving more distant objects, and the sun's vast bath of light laid a hint of rose on the prairie's tawny yellow. The wagon had rolled steadily forward, was by then paralleling the lake at a distance of six or seven miles. But this was not far enough north for it to have been Harry Sands or Fred Downey for some strange reason bringing a wagon out from Prairie.

So strong was his sense of warning by then, he was not greatly surprised when on the low bluff over the creek valley he looked out and saw, directly across from him, a wagon standing beside a camp set up in the trees by the stream. He knew at once what it was, the thing they had all dreaded, and though it was off his patented land it was in the heart of his range, next to the creek on which this part of his range depended.

He sat there weak and sick in the first moment of impact, from which he recovered quickly for, except for his temper, he was a stable, solid man. If that was a nester family, it was a curious one for he saw nothing but grown men, half a dozen. The horses had been unharnessed and tethered, and the men seemed to be fixing a meal at the fire. Al rode to the right until he came to a place where he could drop to the lower level. He cut across to the creek, then turned down toward the camp.

They had seen him by then, were on their feet and waiting, and he saw at a glance that every man there wore a six-shooter while one, in addition, held a rifle. That was not strange considering that these were the first settlers to breach the lake country itself, and they were well advised to be on guard against trouble. Al's face wore a bleak, black look as he rode up to them.

"No use asking what you're going here," he said. "You think you're taking a homestead, but you're wrong. This is my range."

The man with the rifle was big and burly; his legs were long, his arms were long, and so was his body. He looked more like a rangeman than a farmer, although there were no saddle horses about, and his companions were cut to the same pattern. They were the kind of riffraff a man saw in Ogallala and Julesburg, Al thought, and all at once he knew they had been sent there by Gallant.

"This ain't nobody's range any more," the man said. "It's my claim." He made a sweeping motion, up the creek and down, then from bluff to bluff. "A whole section."

"Section?" Al gasped.

The man grinned at him. "That's right. This here's a desert claim. A whole section, not just a quarter. We're going to dam the crick and irrigate it."

That hit harder than the first discovery. "The hell you are!" Al shouted.

"The claim's filed, mister," the man said coolly. "Nothing you can do about it that I know of."

"Who are you, anyhow?"

"The name's Morgan—Jape Morgan. I hired these other men to work for me."

"The hell you did," Al exploded. "You're a pack of gun hands, and Gallant hired the lot of you. It won't work, Morgan. I've grazed this range a long time. I don't aim to let you or anybody else cut it up."

Morgan's stubbled face took on a sneer, his gaze slid around the spread-out circle of watchers. "Gunmen, he calls us. Your name must be Vassey. They said at the land office

51

you've got some land below here. But that don't give you a right to come here and mouth threats and insults. Get out of here, Vassey, before we teach you better manners."

Goaded by the man's cool insolence, Al cried, "You damned buzzards!" then all at once discovered that a man on his left had drawn a gun.

"Get down from that horse, Vassey," the man said.

Al realized too late that he had let them bait him into trouble. He stared flatly, defiantly at the man with the gun and didn't budge.

"Better do what he says," Morgan drawled.

Al swung down recklessly. "If one or all of you thinks he can improve my manners," he returned, "let him have at it." He stood there, thick-necked, thick-shouldered, his feet planted solidly. Few men in the lake country had worn a gun habitually in ten years, but now he wished earnestly that he had one with him. Then he saw them coming at him in a rush.

Al belted out with his right and caught Morgan in the belly, he swung the other way and kicked another man in the crotch. Scooping a handful of dust, he threw it into a third man's face, then somebody jumped him from behind. Wrenching forward, Al threw the fellow over his head, only to be kicked hard in the crotch from behind as he bent. He went down in sick agony, the man behind leaping onto him. Al rolled, numb with pain, too dazed to do anything but wrench and writhe desperately. Somehow he broke free, heard a man curse, but he couldn't get up. Two men had his arms, pulling them straight out. Al heaved his body, but it did no good.

"All right," he heard Morgan panting. "Get him up."

They lifted Al upright, they pulled his arms straight behind him, somebody's foot in the small of his back. A second pain rolled over the first from the stretching, he

52

could barely see. Morgan stepped in and his fists went to work. First they hit Al in the belly, then they hit him in the face. When the man behind let go, Al fell, was completely still for a moment.

Very slowly then he shoved himself to a sitting position. Blood coursed down his chin, one of his eyes was closing already. Morgan and his men stood watching, their faces wore little or no expression. Al let out a groan, then pushed himself to a rocking stand.

"Maybe that'll teach you," Morgan said, "to keep off other people's property unless you can behave."

Al saw his horse standing at what seemed a great distance and he staggered toward it. He barely had the strength to raise himself into the saddle. A man picked up his hat and handed it to him. Al turned the horse and rode on down Red Butte Creek.

Roman Five, like Fishhook and Tack, was a two-bit spread. Its headquarters lay beside the creek, shaded by old riparian trees. Its horse pasture was larger than most and there was a breaking trap. As he rode in to the house, he had ahot coal in his brain that blinded him to everything else. Swinging down at the porch, he stepped across and into the kitchen. A rifle stood in the corner there, and he picked it up. He shifted it to his left hand and used the right to take cartridges out of a box on the shelf above and drop them into his pocket.

So great was the violence that drove him, he was not aware that his mother had wheeled herself into the room until she gave an outcry.

"Albert! What happened to you? What are you doing with that rifle?"

"Never mind."

Ellen Vassey had always been a small woman, now she looked like a child in the chair, that had imprisoned her for five years. Her eyes were large and black-rimmed but curiously, considering her age and suffering, her dark hair was only streaked with gray, her face had not lost all the old beauty he remembered so well. Al could only stare at her.

"It's happened, hasn't it?" she cried. "Home-steaders."

"Don't worry about it. I'll take care of it."

"Not with that rifle, Albert."

He broke his glance away from her, swung to the door, and went out. He heard her call urgently as he sent the horse driving out of the yard. All the years of his life prompted him as he turned back up the creek, starting with the day his father had come here with little more than a wife and child and a few steers. Charlie Vassey had earned an eternal right to this range, a right no one could dispute successfully while his son drew breath.

Al crossed the creek and moved along under the western bench, which was nearer to the Red Butte than the other bluff. He rode swiftly, his compelling urge blinding him even to the day's heat. In some thirty minutes he reined in, swung down, and moved on afoot with the rifle. Because he knew his range so well he came in directly below the camp, moving back across the creek through the rocks and trees, crawling the last few feet without warning of his return. He looked bitterly on a camp that again was indolent while the men there ate the meal he had interrupted before. The trees were thin enough about the camp that he could see all six men. He lay where he had some low rocks for cover.

They were drinking coffee now, smoking and sitting around the fire, the wagon on beyond them. He trained the rifle on the tallest of the figures, which he thought belonged to Morgan. He shot, saw Morgan go over as

54

he jacked the rifle, while men crawled frantically to get protection, using the trees and the wagon. Al shot again without visible results, and by then they had disappeared. That didn't matter; when they recovered from the shock they would know who it was and set out to get him, and they couldn't do that without taking chances.

He settled patiently, the spewing temper that so far had driven him changing to a deadly patience. In a moment a gun cracked viciously, the bullet shrilled off the rock protecting Al, a lucky shot or else a warning that at least one of them had him spotted. Al withheld retaliation but he had himself located a man, who was behind the tree to the right of the campfire. He concentrated on this one, pitting his patience against their impatience, and in a moment he saw the man edge out from behind the tree. Al fired before the man could jerk back; he saw an arm flop into view and then a whole body as a spasm shoved the man out, then down.

Two other guns disputed it, Al heard the bullets on his rock as he pressed flat. It was time to make a change, and he began to push himself backward, still flat, working his body and using his hands and feet. The forward rock protected him enough that he got in behind the big-bored cottonwood on his left without drawing fire. He came to a careful stand, trying to repress the sound of his breathing, then he risked a look.

He could see nothing but the bodies of the men he had hit and hoped no one suspected his change of position. With intent care, the rifle ready, he watched the two low rocks between the still men and the creek. But the first movement he saw was somebody under the wagon. He drove in a shot, and there was no more motion there. Then a bullet tore bark from the cottonwood, something hit him and spun him around. He went over, feeling nothing but an intense, paralyzing cold, his main reaction in that instant a fear that someone had seen him go down.

A less driven man might not have thrown it off, but Al lay there with his will clamped to his objective; he fought back the sick waves and in a moment began to recover. He was still shielded by the trees, there was no charge, and he dared to hope they did not realize what that last shot had done. He discovered that he had been hit in the bulge of his hip, the impact throwing him, the bone-relayed jar momentarily stunning his brain. The blood was soaking his pants, he had no feeling in the leg, let alone control of it. Slowly, but without pain as yet, he worked himself back into position behind the tree.

He could no longer stand, which handicapped him, lowering his perspective until he had little chance of detecting a target unless it showed itself clearly. So he had to wait, and as he waited the wound began to thaw out, at first sending a throbbing pain along his whole side, then adding to that pains so sharp and shooting he nearly cried out. He wanted, in this interlude, to replace the empties in the rifle from the extras in his pocket but feared to try it.

He lay there panting even without exertion, and his determination to free Roman Five of this threat was not a whit diminished. The ranch, if anything, was all the more precious to him, the warm earth that supported him, the air, the sky above. In the odd, short quietude he could hear the murmur of the Red Butte, and his mind went back in the keenest remembrance to his boyhood when sometimes Nora would come to play with him, though rarely since Peyt had always been her special friend. He probably had started loving her then, although the real man's love had not come until later, the hopeless love he had never pressed because she was tied to Peyt and he to his mother.

All at once Al saw a man's hatless head begin to lift from, behind the closest rock, straight ahead of him, and he was again a cool, unfeeling deadliness. The man saw Al and had a choice between ducking or rising on and firing, and he chose the latter. Al shot and saw him throw up his arms, the revolver flying out of a relaxing hand, and then the man went down.

Again came the quietness, the waiting. Al didn't let himself think back any more for his whole life had come into focus in this place and moment. He didn't know what made him look to the left, but suddenly he threw a quick, searching glance toward the creek. The top of its sandy cutbank was grown with weeds and he could see nothing, yet he was worried, a realization coming that one of them could have thrown himself over the bank in the first scramble to get away from the shooting. He was badly placed to cover himself both on that side and ahead, and his paralyzed hip and leg made quick movement impossible.

He began to pant again as he waited, watching two ways now, knowing he had only one or two cartridges left in the rifle, unwilling to tie himself up trying to shove in fresh loads. His palms turned wet with sweat, and all at once a terrible thirst clawed his throat. Nausea hit the pit of his stomach, rolled through him. It was the waiting. Using his elbows, he lifted himself up a little, staring hard across the deserted camp, hunting the merest hint of a man.

Then sound crashed on his left, he jerked his upper body around, and two men swarmed up from the creek, shooting fast. Al fired one shot, then something hit him, and that was the end of the fight.

CHAPTER 6

RYE JONES STARED ACROSS THE SUPPER TABLE AT THE open door, saying, "Somebody's coming, Martha, coming fast." Then he went on eating, a simple, earthy man who enjoyed his body's hungers and its satisfactions. Martha was a good cook, a good wife; she knew how to cater to him all around. He saw her head perk as she listened to the hoof drum grow louder. Then they both rose from the table and walked out to the porch.

Rye recognized Harry Sands from the upper Red Butte and instantly realized that something drove Sands even as Sands drove the blue gelding. Whipping into the yard, Sands flung himself from the saddle as the horse wheeled around in a dust cloud.

Sands' mouth worked, and he said, "God, Rye," and that was all.

"Take it easy," Rye said, putting his hand on Sands' shoulder.

Sands walked to the porch and sat down on its edge, bent forward, his shoulders shaking. "There's been a fight on the Five," he managed to say. "Must have been nesters. They're dead—four of 'em—and Al is, too."

Rye heard Martha's choked cry and sat down hard himself. He stared at Sands' blanched face, which now worked soundlessly.

"Martha," Rye said quietly, "fetch my bottle."

The whisky revived Sands somewhat, took the chalk out of his skin. He shook his head, saying, "I was coming down to borrow a saw from Al, and I come on

58

it. Wagon camp. Two dead men under the wagon, one by the fire, another behind a tree. Al was a good shot. He didn't miss. He was behind another tree. Been shot twice. Hip and head."

"Have you told his mother?"

"It'll kill her. I come here first."

Rye said, "Get ready, Martha. Harry, you take another pull on that bottle."

Rye needed a drink himself, but a hundred things crowded him. He saw Martha's skirt swish as she fled into the house she and Ellen Vassey had always been the best of friends. Because it was second nature, he found his hat, then rushed out to saddle horses, one with a side rig for his wife. By the time he got back to the house with them, Sands was on his feet, the color back in his cheeks. Rye didn't blame him for his reaction— once, years before, he had himself nearly fainted at the smell of blood where men had died violently.

"Harry," he said kindly, "you cut a beeline for Circle C and tell Jim. I'll go to Tack. Martha's the best one to tell Al's mother, and we'll all get there as soon as we can. Maybe I'll come by way of Crown. Sombody'll have to go from there for the sheriff."

He rode east on the south shore road, faster than he liked to ride in recent years. There was a bitter taste in his mouth, as well as the thawing grief in him, for Al, who had grown up with Rye's own boys, still seemed like his own. Deeper lay a slowly stirring fear. He and Martha were old now, they had worked hard all their lives for a small competence, they had seen their two sons destroyed by a prairie fire, they had come to the twilight years that they hoped to spend in peace together at the edge of Silver.

The arrival of Rye Jones at breakneck speed was enough to have Bill Trevers waiting in his yard. Nora had come to the porch and was staring in an intent, strained way.

"What is it, Rye?" Bill said as Rye pulled up. "Something wrong with Martha?"

"No," Rye said, and told them.

Nora stood with her hands pressed to her eyes, Bill's knees loosened and his mouth opened.

"I'm going over there," Nora said, her jaw firming.

"You go along, Bill," Rye said. "I sent Sands across to Jim's. I'm going by Crown. Peyt can send a puncher to Prairie to wire down the railroad for the sheriff. God, Bill, what does it mean?"

"It means Gallant," Bill spat.

"I reckon, but we'll never know. He won't own up to it, and Al cleaned the squatters out. Where's that going to leave Ellen?"

"We'll do what we can for her," Bill said, and headed for the corral to get horses for himself and Nora.

Rye climbed to the Moccasin bench and followed it along the southeastern shore of Silver, high enough he could see the whole lake in the softening light, seeing evil in it now that it had brought bloody contention to the country it had graced so long, served so well. In thirty years of living on the prairie Rye had never ceased to marvel at its ability to destroy men and make them destroy one another.

Crown lay in early darkness when Rye rode in. Punchers sat on the bunkhouse steps, others played poker inside. Rye looked around for Peyt, who called from the shadows of the big house porch.

"That you, Rye? What's up?"

Rye rode over to the edge of the porch and saw Peyt lounging there in a hammock. "Massacre on the Five," he said. "Al's dead, and so's four squatters who tried to set up on the crick."

60

Peyt's feet hit the floor. He rose and walked over, staring.

"You mean that?" he asked.

"It'd be mighty poor joking matter."

"My God."

"Get a man to Prairie to wire the sheriff. I'm going back to Five on the north shore."

"Wait a minute. I'm going with you."

"Suit yourself."

The offer surprised Rye, for Peyt and Al had never got along, no more than had his own boys with Peyt. But death was a shocking, disturbing thing that often lifted men out of pettiness. He saw Peyt leg it for the bunkhouse, where he gave some orders. Then Peyt rushed on to the corral and in a few minutes rode back.

"You say there were four of them?" Peyt said as they rode on together.

"That's what Sands told me. Gallant was behind 'em."

"Not much doubt about that."

"I sure don't know what Ellen's going to do."

"I'll do all I can for her, Rye, any way I can do it."

Jim Carlin rode north at a plunging speed with Harry Sands. He had put in a hard day, had gone to bed when Sands arrived to tell him what had happened. He was still numb, unable to think coherently. He had liked Al, understanding his problems, and there had been the special bond between them of a hopeless longing for Nora.

Fishhook was dark as they passed, curving on around Silver on the north road. Forty minutes later they rode into Roman Five. Bill Trevers sat on the front steps.

"Martha and Nora are in with Ellen," Bill said. "She knew already—that is, she guessed. Al come in. He'd

61

been beat up. He got his rifle and went back. She couldn't stop him."

"Beat up?" Jim asked sharply.

"That's all she knows. Al was clean out of his mind."

"They wanted him to attack," Jim said bitterly. "They were out to get him."

"Thank God, he made 'em pay for it. We might as well go up there." Bill's voice sounded like he did not relish the prospect. He walked out to where his horse was tied to the yard fence and swung up. They headed up the creek through what now was a bright moonlight.

They reached the camp in half an hour. Leaving the horses, they walked in carefully. Jim looked down at the dead man sprawled by the cold fire. Glancing about, he saw the other three. Sands led them down the creek to where Al's body lay behind an old cottonwood. The battered face of the man stared up at them. They took off their hats and stood there through a long moment.

With a gusty sigh, finally, Bill said, "I reckon we better not move him till the law gets here. There'll be questions as to who started it, and all that."

"I'll stay with him," Jim said. "You two go back if you want."

"I reckon I'll stay, too," Bill said.

"I'll be back," Sands said. "But I better get home and tell the missus what kept me." He rode on along the creek.

Jim walked over to the wagon and looked in. "Six bedrolls," he called to Bill, "and I don't see the horses that pulled the wagon."

"You think a couple got away?" Bill asked.

"Looks like it. Somebody had to kill Al after he did these four in. He was shot through the head."

"I hope they're caught," Bill said furiously. "I want to

see them hang."

"They must have come from Prairie. Somebody besides Gallant would know about them. I've got to go over there in the morning. If we can nail them we might sweat them into implicating him."

"He's guilty, all right."

"He's guilty of a lot of things," Jim answered, "and he's still a free man."

They took blankets from the wagon and covered the bodies. They built a fire, for the night's chill was flowing in. They said nothing more to each other.

Nora sat beside the stricken woman she had just helped out of the wheel chair and into bed. She was still amazed at the courage of Ellen Vassey, who had taken the confirmation of her fears in dry-eyed shock. Now Ellen lay with her eyes closed, and Nora was acutely conscious of the tortured body that could neither stand nor lie straightened out, and she remembered vividly what a fine, straight figure Ellen had had six short years back. Life was so intensely cruel, even without such things as had happened that day on the Five.

Ellen quite suddenly opened her eyes and said, as if it trailed a thought. "He loved you, Nora."

"I know he did."

"He was a good boy."

"I never knew one better," Nora said. "Don't think about him now."

Out in the kitchen Martha, in her brisk way, was fixing a supper that she knew quite well Ellen would not eat. Nora sat thinking of the two women who, next to Bill, had been her substitute mothers through most of her life, remembering what a close-knit community the lake country had always been, like they were all one family.

Then the Jones boys had been killed, and now Al, and she was frightened, for only Peyt and herself were left of the younger ones, while~the old were getting weak and crippled by age at a time when they had to fight, perhaps for their very lives. Tantro and Sands and Downey were good men, but for some odd reason she was glad that Jim Carlin had come to live in the country.

She had been shocked when Lagg had tried to kill Jim and been killed by him. Although she had been glad of Jim's escape, his invincibility and capacity for ruinous retaliation had only deepened her feeling of his hardness, of the danger in him. She had been glad once that Peyt had none of that quality in him, and now she wondered why Jim's possession of it all at once made his presence a comfort to her.

Martha came in with soup that Ellen refused, so Martha sat down beside the bed, and Nora slipped out. Going to the front porch, she sat down, seeing through the moonlight the glint of Silver down past the trees. She wanted to cry, yet could not, and she didn't want to keep thinking back the way she did. Life lay ahead, it couldn't exist anywhere else now, and in another two months or less she and Peyt would be married.

Perhaps it was her tiredness but she got no lift at all now from that prospect. Instead she sat like this with the guilty thought of Jim in her mind because she had heard him speak, just once and briefly, a while ago out here. Her thoughts, perversely turning backward again, went to what Jim had said that day when Bill so transparently had him come by the house, the remark about her being afraid to trade a lifelong affection for what might prove to be a new, real love. There was no question she was afraid now, she had been afraid that day because of the nester trouble, but it could not be more than that when it

64

seemed so right, so sweet and natural for her and Peyt to keep on spending their lives together.

When she saw horsemen riding in from the east she knew that someone had come from Crown with Rye, she knew it was Peyt and was glad for she needed him. They rode into the yard quietly and swung down before her. She didn't rise, although she yearned for Peyt's arms around her, for they were both shy about showing affection before others.

"Bad news," Peyt said as he bent down and touched his lips to her hair. "How is she?"

Reaching up, Nora caught his hand and held it. "All right. She's endured so much, I guess nothing can hurt her much more."

"I want to help her," Peyt said earnestly, "and it'll be awkward with her remembering how it always was with me and Al. Will you come in with me to see her?"

"Why, of course," she said, rising to her feet.

"Where's the men?" Rye asked.

"They went up the creek."

"Reckon I'll go up there, too," Rye said, and rode on.

Nora walked into the house with Peyt and took him on into Ellen's bedroom. Martha looked up in surprise when she saw who was with her. Walking over to the bed, Peyt looked down at Ellen.

He said, "I wanted to tell you not to worry. My boys can look after the Five and they will."

Surprise showed faintly on Ellen's face. After a thoughtful moment she said, "That's good of you, Peyt."

"I've got to tell you," he said in a rushing way, "how I wish Al and me had got along better. We just rubbed each other the wrong way."

She didn't answer.

Nora was proud of Peyt as she went out with him. He

65

said he was going on up the creek, so she returned to the porch. There was some good in adversity, and this emergency had made him see his responsibility and rise to it. She was glad he had done it without coaxing. Boyd, with the complacency some men have about their longevity, had not prepared Peyt for the job of running Crown. She was surprised that she should feel so much relief that he was coming through all right.

Martha came out after a while and seated herself on the step beside Nora, saying, "She's asleep finally. That was good of Peyt, and I don't mind saying it nearly floored me. He's going to be all right."

"I've never doubted it," Nora said, and all at once wondered why she had needed to say that at all.

"He's lucky. Not many men have a woman with the faith you've got."

"You sound like it takes more than usual with Peyt."

"Doesn't it?" Martha said softly.

CHAPTER 7

WHEN DAYLIGHT CAME TO THE RED BUTTE, JIM WAS alone at the squatter camp, the others having gone down to the Five's headquarters to get some breakfast and see what work needed immediate attention. As soon as the light was strong enough, Jim looked the scene over more carefully. He had removed the bedding, but the wagon still held a plow, a number of picks, shovels, and other tools, groceries and some gum boots, and something more that told him a good deal, an earth-moving slip such as he had used in ditching and diking the sink. All at once he looked about with bright interest, seeing the flatness of the land, the whole of which had a slight fall to the south all the way to the lake. He soon understood what had brought the squatters here, a little of which Al must have learned from them to be aroused so fully. A desert claim would be big enough to take this whole section away from him.

All at once Jim swung and stared hard to the east, seeing a party of eight or ten riders break out of the canyon that bisected the bluffs and come directly toward him. In a couple of minutes a trotting team emerged, drawing a hack. He dropped down from the wagon and stood staring at them rubbing the raspy line of his jaw. They came steadily on, seeming to know where they were going, then a moment later he saw the glint of metal on the lead rider's vest and recognized Bob Landorf, the county sheriff.

A deep frown stood on Jim's face as they reached him, Landorf and two other men dressed like rangemen, the rest a bobtail detachment he knew had come out from Prairie. The swift-moving hack, keeping up, pulled in behind, and he saw Dr. Winthrop, who was the coroner.

"You got here damned fast," Jim said to the sheriff. "We didn't get a wire off to you till last night."

Landorf was a heavy, middle-aged man with a hard but open face. "I got a wire yesterday noon," he answered, tipping a nod. "From them. I come over to Prairie on the afternoon train."

Jim swung a quick, fierce look at the other two plainsmen. "So you're the pair that got away."

"Now, Jim," the sheriff said quickly, "there's been trouble enough already. It's not that I don't see Vassey's side, but he was clean off base. Jape Morgan filed on this section—I checked that with the land office—and he come out here to work it. Vassey shot up his camp

67

and killed four of them. These two got away and sent for me. I brought men so we can hold the inquest here where it happened."

"Which one of you's Morgan?" Jim shot at the pair.

One gave him a hostile stare and said, "Jape was the first one Vassey killed."

"You know anything about the case, Jim?" Landorf asked.

"Only what Ellen Vassey said. Al come in beat up, got his rifle, and left again. That's all she knows."

"Well, I won't bring her up here to testify. Did you say beat up?"

"That's what she said. You can look at Al and see for yourself."

"You know anything about that, Rankin?" Landorf asked the hard-eyed man who seemed to lead the pair.

"Not me."

"You, Quigley?"

The other man shook his head.

Jim moved off by himself while the sheriff and coroner took care of the legal formalities. The Prairie men brought along for a jury walked solemnly about the scene of the fight. Rankin still talked for the two survivors, pointing around to explain what he said. They had been fixing their noon meal early, he said, so they could get to work right afterward, then all hell broke loose. The first shot killed Morgan. One by one Vassey had picked off three more men. Rankin and Quigley had managed to get into the creek bed and, using its bank to protect them, move up on Vassey's flank. As they closed in, he noticed them and started shooting again. Rankin had to kill him.

The verdict was predictable, even had the jury not been comprised of men from Prairie. Four men had come to their deaths by murder, whether or not it was an aggravated assault—the death of Vassey was justified.

Afterward, when they began to load the bodies, Jim stepped up to Landorf. "I'm claiming Al's. Leave it here."

The sheriff nodded and remained behind when the others pulled out, Rankin and Quigley leaving with them. Afterward Landorf walked over to the wagon tongue and sat down, pulling off his hat.

"A bad business, Jim," he said. "I used to run cattle, but we can't stop change. You only have to look at Al to see he'd been beat up, but he was still off base. I know how this little patch that's left of the cow country must feel about it. The settlers see only the other side of it. This thing's stirred up a lot of feeling in Prairie. They're liable to organize another Homesteaders' Protective Association, like they did farther east. If that happens, it's good-by to you folks."

"But this thing was murder," Jim said angrily. "I told you all about Gallant when Lagg tried for me. That coneroo knew what a hothead Al was. He sent Morgan here to bait Al into something like this, with men enough to see Morgan put it over."

"Considering how it come about, I still can't touch him. I'll stay here if you want to go down to Five and send up a rig for Al."

Nodding, Jim got his horse and rode down the creek. Bill and Rye were sitting on the corral fence when he reached there. They told him Peyt had returned to Crown but would, send a couple of men over to stay, doing the work. They seemed a little impressed by that fact, although it made no impact on Jim at all.

He told them that the sheriff was at the squatter camp, that the inquest had already been held, that Gallant could not be touched although he undoubtedly had got away with murder.

"Well, Al did some good," Rye said bitterly. "He
69

vacated that claim with the first shot—the one that killed Morgan. You think the other two will try to hold onto it, Jim?"

"Not unless they get a bigger crew than Morgan had. They don't look tough enough. Anyhow, they were only there to kill Al."

"But why?"

"Mrs. Vassey can't stay here and run the Five. That's obvious to anybody who knows her physical condition."

"Ah," Bill said. "And Gallant thinks he can buy it now."

"And what can she do but sell to him?" Jim asked. "Where's there a buyer for a cattle ranch being cut up by homesteaders? If there was one, besides Gallant, what kind of a price would he pay under such circumstances?"

"Well, let's take the buckboard up, Bill," Rye said wearily, "and bring her boy home. She wants him buried beside Charlie, up on the knoll, Jim. Me and Bill dug the grave this morning."

Jim walked toward the house. When he stepped onto the porch he saw Nora in the kitchen, and to his surprise she had a tired, sad, but friendly smile for him. As he walked on in, she said, "Don't you want some breakfast, Jim?"

He made a wry face. "I couldn't eat a thing, Nora. I want to see Mrs. Vassey."

"She was asleep a moment ago. Let me give you something."

"All right."

He went outdoors, hung up his hat, and scrubbed up. When he moved back inside, Nora had put food and coffee on the table for him. Suddenly she said, "Jim, why do things like this have to happen?"

"To make somebody money, this time."

"But who could it profit?"

"Gallant wants this place," Jim said as he began to eat.

70

"And he's probably the only one who would buy it."

"Peyt could," she said promptly, "and he would to upset Gallant. I'm going to speak to him about it."

Jim stared at her curiously but said nothing.

Once he started eating his appetite came back, and he made a meal of it. He rolled a cigarette and accepted a second cup of coffee, aware of her presence as she came near to pour it, still poignantly aware as she moved away again.

He said, "Peyt's turned into a wonder boy all at once. Solving all the problems."

She swung and looked at him, her dark eyes flashing. "Why, Jim, that sounds small."

"Probably is small. I've never claimed to like him. Even if I saw cause, which I don't, I wouldn't dare because I want his girl."

"You know I won't let you talk to me like that."

"Won't let yourself listen, you mean," he corrected.

She flushed. "Jim, it isn't decent for you to keep after me this way."

"It isn't decent for a woman to marry her own son."

She stared in horror. "What made you say that?" she asked in a choked voice.

"Because that's all that's between you. I think you guess it yourself, or you wouldn't have turned so red in the face."

Martha came in from the other room. "Ellen's awake now," she said, "and promised to eat a little."

"Wonder if I could see her first?" Jim asked.

"Sure. Go on in."

A moment later, when he looked down at Ellen, Jim found it hard to say what he wanted. "We all feel mighty bad about it," he began, "and we want to help any way we can. Seems I heard you were a

71

schoolteacher once."

The woman's eyes turned misty. "Yes. I had a school when I met my husband."

"Well, I would have mentioned it before," Jim said, "but Al was proud and wanted to do things for himself. But I've got a brother in Arizona. They live way out, and I know they'd like to have you come and stay with them winters and teach their kids. The woman's done what she can but never had much schooling, and their young ones growing up that way worries them both."

Her twisted hand came up to touch his. "That's nice of you, Jim, but I've got to be near a doctor."

He saw at once that she knew he would have to arrange it with his brother, probably paying her board and using the teaching to cover her pride. "Why don't you try it one winter?" he asked urgently. "Maybe it would help you enough you could come back to Five."

"I'd like to come back sometime," Ellen said, "but I've got to sell now, Jim. There's no other way. The Five doesn't pay enough to let me hire a man to run it, or for somebody to rent it, either. You're a fine man. Al thought a lot of you."

"I'm proud to hear it. He proved himself up there, and that's something you can always be proud of."

"I am. It was so foolish—yet so like his father."

"The breed's disappearing."

She looked up at him with eyes clouded and pained. "Everything is—everything that was so strong and fine and good."

"It sure looks like it, sometimes."

Jim got his horse and rode out on the north shore road. He stopped at Fishhook to pump water for the in-stock, since Rye had been away quite a while. He

72

stopped for the same purpose at Tack, then rode on south toward Circle C. He was jaded, his feeling spent with an aftermath that was bleak and wearing.

When he came to the edge of the sink he stopped his horse and looked across the fertile depression that represented the hardest years of his life. It all pressed in on him now, the full meaning of what had happened across the lake. Gallant would have Roman Five, there seemed to be no way to prevent it, and he would go on around the lake until he had it and could dam the Dry, when Circle C would go. He was no more concerned for his ranch than for the others; it was just intolerable to have to sit and let things happen because the law was all on the side of their enemies.

CHAPTER 8

AFTER THE LITTLE PROCESSION CAME DOWN THE HILL above the Vassey house it began to break up. Fred Downey rode out for the upper Red Butte with the Sands family. The Crown riders, except for Tex Rinehart, whom Peyt had told to stay behind, headed along the north shore for Crown. Rye and Martha Jones, Bill accompanying them, took the west road, depressed, worried, and saddened. Nora had gone into the house with the grief-stricken mother, whose wheel chair the men had pushed up the hill then brought carefully down again. Peyt stood on the porch with Jim Carlin, wondering with annoyance why Jim hadn't left when the others did.

Peyt was aware that Jim sensed more than most men would have guessed, and this faculty for being so prompt and right was one of the things about the tall,

73

dark man that fed Peyt's dislike. He was intensely curious as to why Jim lingered, almost as if he meant to prevent what Peyt wanted to do.

Trying to sound casual, Peyt said, "Well, I guess that winds it up, Jim. See you later." The hostility that had flared between them in Prairie had been put down for this occasion, although Peyt knew it simmered in Jim as much as in himself, that there was no use trying to excuse his presence in Gallant's office that day. There was no use building up the animosity and suspicion, either. He walked off toward the barn.

Tex Rinehart, who had replaced Gordon as Crown's foreman, waited at the corral. He was a younger man than Guy, tall, red-haired, and sardonic. But he had filled the job well, to Peyt's relief, and would fit better yet with what was coming. Peyt knew there were blank pages in Tex's past, but that did not trouble him. It helped to know that another man was vulnerable.

They rose to saddle and rode up the creek, saying nothing. Where the road crossed the stream, and when they were screened from the house by the trees, Peyt halted and swung down. Moving back across on the steppingstones at the ford, he placed himself where he could watch the house. Jim still stood on the back porch, leaning against a post. Presently Nora appeared in the doorway, then stepped on out. Peyt had to know whether it was she Jim wanted to see, and this had been the only way he could think of to hurry it up and get rid of him.

Yet he felt a strong antagonism riffle up his spine as he watched them there so close together. He had had this deep, possessive attitude toward her as far back as he could remember, was aware of Jim's feeling for her, and whenever the vaguest thought of her turning to Jim or any other man trailed across his mind he had a reaction close to terror. She had always been of supreme importance to him, without her he was nothing at all.

The fear of her learning too much, through Jim or her own insight, was the only thing to detract from his pleasure in the new life that had opened for him at the instant in which Boyd Peyton drew his last gasping breath. His need for her was greater than any other he'd ever felt, and the strength of his love for her was in the fact that she understood and never failed him. It began so long ago he could not remember the first time she had relieved him of the unbearable feelings that by some mischance were the very essence of his nature, and it struck him now that this act of relieving was also an essential part of hers, a womanliness sprung prematurely in a small girl's breast.

Jim talked with Nora quite a while, and she waited on the porch when finally he walked out to his horse and rode away on the west road, her eyes following him. Peyt went, back to where Tex stood by his horse, smoking a cigarette, enraged that she should show any interest at all in another man.

Tex said, "We going somewhere or just killing time?"

"Both," Peyt answered.

They rode on to the squatter camp, where Morgan's wagon still stood in the morning heat. Pausing there, Tex looked around with interest. "Vassey sure shot it up," he commented.

"Committing suicide," Peyt said complacently. His worry was leaving him; he had always been able to handle Nora, he could again. An eagerness came to him and he added, "We'll go on up the crick later," and swung his horse. Tex shrugged his shoulders, then turned and followed him.

Nora was in the kitchen when presently Peyt walked in. He saw nothing on her face to disturb him and said, "The nester wagon's still up there. I hope that doesn't mean one of the others intends to file." It was the first time they had been alone in several days and, moving on to her, he took her in his arms. He heard her tired sigh as she turned up her mouth to him. It struck him that there was never any fire in their kisses, only tenderness and comforting, taken and given. In a way, the thought of possessing her as a woman was offensive to him, although once they were used to that it would seem more natural.

When they stepped apart, he took a cup off a hook and poured himself coffee. Seated at the table, he rolled a cigarette. She took coffee for herself and came to join him, and a pleasantness came over him at the thought that soon they would be living together on Crown with her always near him.

Bluntly he said, "What did Jim want to see you about?"

She searched his face quickly. "He doesn't like something I suggested yesterday about Ellen. I shouldn't have done it, but it popped out. It's obvious she'll have to sell the Five, and Gallant's the only one who'd buy it under the circumstances. Unless you could and would to keep it out of his hands as well as to help her out of a terrible situation."

"Me?" Peyt gasped.

"I didn't mention it to her—only to Jim."

"It's no wonder he wouldn't like such an idea. The others wouldn't, either, and I wouldn't blame them. It would look like I was taking advantage of Ellen's misfortunes."

He shrugged. "Well, what did Jim say?"

She looked away from him. "It's just the prejudice little outfits have against big ones getting bigger. But it's better than Gallant's getting hold of it."

"You must have told him that. What did he say?"

"He just shrugged. But something's got to be done, Peyt. Would you consider it?"

"But, golly," Peyt said, "what would I do with it?"

"Isn't it useful enough to keep Gallant from getting lake frontage?"

"How could I make Ellen understand?"

"She hates the thought of being forced to sell to Gallant. Tell her frankly why you want it."

Serenity was back in Peyt, although he showed her nothing but a continuing dubiety. He had been deeply uneasy as to whether he could make it look right to Nora, and now she had suggested it herself. He didn't care what anyone else thought, not even Bill, as long as it sat well with Nora.

"I might feel her out about it," he conceded finally.

"Oh, will you? She was resting, but I'll see if she's awake."

When Nora had gone into the other room, Peyt let himself smile. Expansive and relaxed, he got another cup of coffee, rolled a second cigarette. Presently he heard the sound of the wheel chair trundling across the floor. It appeared in the doorway, Ellen in it, Nora behind. Nora pushed the crippled woman to the table, poured her coffee, then took seat herself. She looked happy.

"What did Al plan for you to do next winter?" Peyt asked guardedly.

"It depended on the money," Ellen said with a tired sigh.

"Would you let me loan it to you?"

She showed an open surprise. "On what security? A

ranch I can't run, maybe can't even sell? Thank you, Peyt, but Al got his pride from his parents. I'll pay my own way if I can."

"Gallant would buy the Five. That's what he wants. He's the only one that would, right now."

"But what can I do?" she cried, holding up her twisted hands.

"Let me take it off your hands. It'd be worth it to stop him."

Ellen gave him the closest kind of scrutiny through a long moment. Then, "Are you sure it wouldn't just be an act of charity on your part?"

"Of course not," he said angrily. "If Gallant gets on the lake, we're a lot worse off than we are now. Besides, the Five joins Crown. I could work it into my own range. You said Al got his pride from his parents. Well, I got something from my father—plain business sense."

Ellen looked uncertainly at Nora. "What do you think?"

"That it would be the best thing for both of you," Nora said promptly.

"Supposing," Peyt said, "that you give me an option right away. That's enough to stop another move from Gallant. Then we could get a fair appraisal made, have the papers drawn up, and all that. It would relieve your worries and mine right now. What do you think of that?"

Suddenly Ellen brought her crippled hands to her face. "I don't want to sell, but I've got to. All right, Peyt, and hurry before I lose my courage."

Nora looked at her with compassion, then found paper and pen and brought them to Peyt. He wrote up a simple option agreement, then called in Tex Rinehart so Tex and Nora could witness it and make certain the thing would be valid any time, anywhere. The period was thirty days, with a provision for renewal although he was certain he could have the ranch in his own name before that time was up. The consideration was generous, and he gave Ellen a check. Her relief was evident with the accomplished fact; only then was Peyt sure of how tightly pressed Al had been for money, of the plight she had been caught in by his death.

"I'll go to the bank tomorrow," Peyt said, "and get the deal started. Then I'll drop in and let Gallant know where he stands."

Presently he and Tex Rinehart were riding up the creek again. Tex had his twisted smile on his face. "So you bought another ranch," he commented.

"Looked like it, didn't it?"

"What're we going to do with it?"

"Make it a mighty important part of Crown. That's what I'm going to show you, because from here on I need your help."

They passed the deserted homestead camp without stopping. Although it was not yet noon, heat lay thickly on the land, deepening its burned look, rendering out its wild smells.

"That Morgan had the right idea," Tex said. "This would make hayland as good as Carlin's if it was watered."

"That's what it's going to be. We could winter a lot more steers that way."

"You ain't worried about squatters any more?"

Peyt didn't answer immediately. They rode on silently, coming at last to the land crown just below Lazy S. Stopping there, Peyt pointed down to where a small huddle of buildings stood by the upper creek, among the trees.

"That," he said, "will be a line camp."

"Lazy S? Now wait a minute. The Five used to use this range, but Sands homesteaded his headquarters, and the Vasseys let him stay."

"They didn't need so much range, but I do, and there's that prior claim. I bought it with the Five, I'll put it back in effect."

"You mean," Tex gasped, "that you're going to run Sands off?"

"We are," Peyt corrected. "And we're going to get Downey off the east fork. We've got to, Tex, to protect ourselves. I'm sending to Sidney for more men. We've got to have them all along the creek. Gallant won't try again, but there's still stray homesteaders to worry about. If any show up, we'll be ready for them."

"Suits me fine," Tex said, his pale eyes gleaming. "But how do we run off Sands and Downey?"

"You'll get your orders," Peyt said, "when you need them."

He sent Tex home from there, telling him to send a couple of men to take over the Five's work. He would have Nora take Ellen to Tack to stay until she left the country so the men could use the house. That eventually would give him three line camps that could hold the north side of Silver against all comers, a base that would be useful when Crown extended its interests on around the west end and back on the south shore to the home ranch.

As he rode down the Red Butte he was pleased to remember that Nora had helped him more than she would ever know. When again he moved he would see to it that she saw things the way he wanted. He knew that would get harder to do, yet he could not stop now. He need not, for luck was surely with him, not only in the swift way Al had ridden into the trap, but in Nora's eagerness for the thing Peyt had already intended to do.

At the start it had bothered him that, because of her, he had to play a hidden role. Now he preferred that, matching his wits against the combined brains of the others, including Gallant, who would cut him down in a minute if he saw a chance. That did a great deal to relieve the nagging shame he had always felt. Whatever he had said or done to defend his father, he had known from boyhood that Boyd was what they claimed, a natural coward. That was the only characteristic in him Peyt himself had despised. Years ago, as Crown grew bigger and stronger, it could have taken over the entire lake country. Boyd had wanted to do it, when he was no longer weak enough to need his neighbors, but he had lacked the courage. The son had the courage, and the proof of it in these last few weeks had made a new man of him.

CHAPTER 9

WHEN BILL TREVERS DREW NEAR THE FIVE HE GOT stage fright, but rode on steadily. Nora had seen him coming and stood on the porch as he came in. She called, "Hello. Have you had your breakfast?"

"Of course I had breakfast," Bill said testily as he rode on up. "Don't forget I cooked for you before you were big enough to do it for me."

He swung down, trailed reins, and climbed the steps. He saw that she was more relaxed than she had been the day before and hoped that meant Ellen felt better. Aware that she expected him to sit down and talk with her, he said, "I've got to see Ellen, and right now. You go fish in the lake or something."

She gave him a startled glance, then shrugged. Afraid that his nerve would fail him, Bill walked into the house, pulling off his old hat. Ellen was seated in her wheel chair by the window; she looked at him in surprise.

"Lonesome, Bill?" she asked. "Or is something wrong?"

"Something's right," Bill said. "I've worked up the nerve to tell you what I've tried to say before. I want you to marry me, Ellen, want it more than anything else."

Her mouth dropped open, her hands lifted and fell back in her lap. "Bill," she breathed, almost in protest, or so it seemed to him in his great urgency.

"I know it's pretty soon after Al's going," he said doggedly, "but while you had him I didn't figure you'd look at an old fellow like me. Now it's different, you're making plans, and I had to speak."

"But, Bill," she protested, "what would any man want with me?"

"Ellen, you cut that out," he said sternly. "What's wrong with you can be fixed. I've wanted to help, but Al prided himself on taking care of you. It'd be my pride now, if you'd let me. I know you're thinking of selling the Five. I don't want that, nobody does. I want to move here and run it. Jim Carlin would be glad to lease Tack."

"You don't understand, Bill. I can't live here."

"The shape you're in now," Bill retorted. "There's Hot Springs, up in the Black Hills, almost next door. You could winter there and summer here till you're well enough to live here all the time."

"But that's so expensive, Bill—the treatments and everything. The Five doesn't make that kind of money, and I wouldn't marry you just to have you foot my bills."

Desperately Bill said, "Can't I make you see what it means to me? What have either of us got to live for if we don't do something like that to help ourselves? I was luckier than Charlie and Al. I've got money put away. Nothing it could buy would be as good as having you as pert and spry as you used to be. Next to Lucy, you were the prettiest woman in the country, the finest, and—well, the one I liked most."

"God bless you, Bill, but it's impossible."

"Do you want to stay here or don't you?"

"I want to terribly, but I gave Peyt an option yesterday."

Bill could only stand and stare at her, disbelieving at first then knowing it was true.

"Why Peyt?" he gasped. "What does he want with it?"

"He knew the only other prospect was Gallant, which practically forced him to buy it himself."

"Well, he'll let you out of it," Bill decided. "He's got to."

"I suppose he would, but I'm not going to take advantage of you."

What did a man dried to gristle and rawhide say to a woman he wanted? The best Bill could do was stare at her with pleading eyes. He was sweating, his tongue was all at once glued to his palate. Suddenly the expression on his face seemed to move her, for she spoke again.

"It's not you, Bill. Next to Charlie, you're as fine a man as I ever knew. You're going to be lonely with Nora gone, I know that. I'd like living with you—if I was pert and spry again. If I get well, Bill, I'll come back. To Tack."

"But there's no need for you to sell the Five. It's

"He was down last night and said so."

"Was this his idea?"

"Well," Bill said sheepishly, "all I needed was a nudge."

"Well, what do you know," Nora said wonderingly. "If you can stay here awhile, I'll go over to Crown right now. I talked Peyt into it. He'll probably jump at the chance to get out of it."

"You're happy about it?" he asked.

"Very. The only thing wrong with my getting married was leaving you to live by yourself. Now I'll even have a mother. Peyt and I both will. Oh, Dad!" Suddenly she was crying in his arms, but they were happy tears, Bill knew.

Peyt was starting for Prairie, following the east shore, when Nora broke out of the trees ahead. The shock of seeing herthere in the sunlight sent fear worming through him. He lifted the gait of his horse as he saw her spur hers. The thought flashing through his mind was that something had happened to Ellen—if she died before the ranch sale was completed everything would be spoiled. He was on his way to see a lawyer, to go to the bank and get things moving.

"What now?" he called as they came together.

To his enormous relief, she smiled at him. "Good news this time," she reported. "You won't have to buy the Five. Dad and Ellen are going to get married and live there."

"Get married?" he gasped.

"Isn't it a surprise?" she said in a happy rush. "Dad wants to run it and turn Tack over to Jim. Can you imagine Jim as a matchmaker? But Dad says all he needed was a little nudge, which Jim gave him. Oh, Peyt, I'm so relieved. Ellen's been unhappy about selling out, even if she's tried to hide it."

Peyt felt as if he had been hit with a sledge hammer, it took work to keep the effect from showing on his face. "So Jim played Cupid," he breathed.

"He was just trying to find a way to help her."

"It happens," Peyt said savagely, "that I've got an option on the Five. Remember?"

She stared at him in deep wonder. "Of course, and you can tear it up. That's the point. It was my silly idea, and if I'd just waited—Peyt, what's the matter? Aren't you happy about it?"

"What's up Carlin's sleeve?" he evaded. "What's he want on Tack for? That might be as bad as having Gallant get hold of Five."

"Why, I certainly see no reason to be suspicious of Jim."

He stared at her hotly. "He always stacked up real high with you, didn't he?"

"What on earth's gone wrong with you, Peyt?"

He realized he had to get hold of his emotions, although the prospect she had laid open appalled him. Putting down his resentment; he said, "You sold me the idea of buying Five, and now I'm for it. It's a sure way to stop Gallant. Besides, my range is closer to the nesters than anybody's. If they start to cut it up, I'll have to pull back. Having Five would allow that. Once Bill's gone and Tack's yours, there'll be range on the other side of the lake, too. I'm thinking of your future as much as mine because we'll have settlers worrying us from here on."

"Dad wouldn't have to sell. He could just lease to Jim."

"But why can't things stand as they are?"

"Because of Dad and Ellen," she cried. "Don't you want them to be happy?"

"Of course I do. But they could live on Tack just as well."

86

"But Ellen doesn't want to sell Five," Nora protested. "She came there as a bride, had her baby in that house, her husband and son are buried on the place. Dad understands what it means to her. So do I, and I want you to give me that option to take back to them. I brought the check you gave her."

Peyt saw that she meant it, knew from experience that once she had made up her mind she was hard to sway. A sick despair filled him. Everything had come so quickly, so opportunely, and now it was going in the same swift, unforeseeable way. The best he could do was stall for time to figure a way around this.

"Look," he pleaded, "that option's all to the good. It shows Gallant he has no chance to get Roman Five. I intend to tell him as much today. Let's let it run on out. If Bill goes on Five he'll be subject to Gallant's dirty work, you know."

"Peyt, it will cloud their future unless they know you can't force a deal through."

"Force one through?" he gasped. "Do you think I'd do that?

"I don't understand why you want to keep the option."

"But I just explained it!"

"It seems to me," Nora said coolly, "that more range to protect Crown is as important to you as checking Gallant."

He threw up his hands, he looked shocked, offended, but it did no good. He had a dreadful moment of uncertainty then, for it was the first time she had failed to support him. "Buying Five never entered my head," he blazed, "until you brought it up. There's still Carlin. Maybe you trust him, but I don't. I don't want him next to Crown, whether he owns Tack or leases it. Let me think it over at least, I'll come over to see you tonight."

"All right," she said dismally.

He rode with her to the end of the lake, where they kissed briefly and only because he pressed for it. Then she turned west.

Once he was alone, heading on toward Prairie, the full fear came to him. He wouldn't turn back, he couldn't, and already he was on dangerous ground with Nora. His face made a bitter twist when he remembered how neatly she had fallen in line with his plans.

He was aware of the unconcealed hostility in Prairie as he rode in and drew up before the new bank, a reminder of how adversely affected the people here had been by what would appear to them to be a massacre of their own kind on the Red Butte. He was a cattleman, as quickly recognizable by his garb as they were, and to them there was no differentiating between individuals. This did not disturb him, in fact it might prove useful to have them aroused so strongly. He left the option at the bank with Crown's other papers, emerged, and took the stairs to Gallant's office.

The promoter was leaning back in his chair, smoking a cigar moodily, but he brought his feet off the desk hurriedly when Peyt walked in.

"I thought your claim stunt would be too slow," he said. "But I was wrong. How soon do you think I should approach the Vassey woman?"

"The Five still isn't on the market," Peyt said. "Bill Trevers is going to marry her and live there. Carlin wants to take over Tack."

Gallant looked stricken. "You don't mean it."

Peyt smiled. "Sorry. But Nora was at Crown before I left, and that's what she told me. We're back where we started, aren't we?"

"It can't happen!" Gallant exploded. "I can't keep on marking time!"

"Any ideas?"

"Damn it, no."

"Neither have I." Peyt began to roll a cigarette. "And I had a real pipe dream, Gallant. Do you know that if the Dry mouth was dammed it would pool a lot of water? You could sell off this whole desert, not just the piddling tract you've got laid out."

"Of course I know it," Gallant retorted. "Also that Trevers owns the mouth of the Dry."

"So he does," Peyt agreed amiably. "I said it was a pipe dream. Pity, though. The thing could be a real money-maker with a dam like that. Bigger market for land, Prairie a lot bigger town. But Bill wouldn't listen, at least to the idea of you running it. He lost what faith he had in you the night Carlin upset your wagon."

"Trevers won't live forever," Gallant said furiously, and all at once he stopped and took a deep breath. "It just happens that your future wife is his only heir."

"What's that got to do with it?"

"Nothing at all." Gallant was calmer, he was almost smiling. "But it occurs to me that if Carlin acquires Tack you'll be out range you expect to inherit through your wife. Too bad Trevers can't be talked out of his desire to marry Mrs. Vassey."

"He can't be," Peyt said.

"I know that, and I'm glad you dropped in."

"Don't see where I helped any," Peyt said, and walked out.

His mind was at ease as he moved across to his horse, mounted, and rode out of Prairie. He would tell Nora that evening that he had seen Gallant only to have the Five threatened again, that the option simply had to run on for Bill's protection. He had a feeling that this was enough, that the matter would soon be taken care of without further effort on his part.

There was mail in Moccasin for Bill Trevers, and Jim Carlin picked it up. He had come to town for tobacco and his own mail, and when the postmaster gave him the letter for Bill he decided on the longer ride home by the main lake road, which would take him past Tack. The late July days were uniformly hot, the summer was far enough along that the dryness of the land all about was at once apparent.

He rode at an easy jog, thinking of last week's funeral, which had impressed him heavily as the tolling of a bell on the end of an era. The old could go out with it much easier than the younger ones brought up to the old ways yet compelled to live in changing times, and it was a pity the change could not have waited until the founders of the cattle business had died decently and at peace.

He was halfway to the lake when he came upon cattle sign. The graze was Tack's, and while it was not unusual for a steer to cross the unfenced road, he saw stitched on the dust the tracks of half a dozen animals too closely bunched to be anything but a cut that had been driven. Before riding over the tracks, he reined in and swung down for a better look. His eyes narrowed when he saw the tracks of a horse overlaid on the others.

For a second he stood staring into the eastward heat, seeing nothing but simmering, empty range. Going back to saddle, he turned the horse and began to follow the cow sign. The clear imprint of the tracks in the dust of the road had not been eroded, which meant they were fairly fresh. He rode with a sudden tension between his shoulders, for rustling this close in had not happened in

90

his time in the lake region. Yet it always began where there were homesteaders in any number, it was axiomatic with that class that they lived the first year on free local beef.

No effort had been made to hide these tracks, they continued due east toward the farm country, which was a matter of supreme insolence or surprising idiocy. He was still on the flattened part of the vast Moccasin bench, enabled by the bold sign to ride at a stiff trot. Presently he could see far forward the first chop hills that marked the edge of the new settlements. He was puzzled, wary, not certain that he was not being led deliberately into some kind of trouble.

He gave the first outlying ridges a close inspection before he rode on through the gap bisecting them. Only a little later he quickly pulled up his horse. He had come in upon one of the region's small, tepid lakes that were kept replenished by the rains. A few trees stood along its edges, nothing else showing but the bare, encircling little hogbacks. The cut of steers had been allowed to loosen up as it came into this place. A rider had gone straight forward to the edge of the lake, and Jim followed those tracks.

As he came in close to the big old tree on the bank he instantly observed open signs of butchering. The offal apparently had been thrown into the water to sink, which had by no means covered the evidence or the smell or the rope mark on a big limb that hung out from the tree. Moreover, there were glaring wagon tracks that came in from the other direction, showing where the vehicle had been turned around then driven out again. Under the tree he could make out the boot prints of two men, the one who had brought in the cattle and the man who had met him here with the wagon and helped with

91

the butchering.

Swearing hotly at the open effrontery, Jim followed the wagon tracks deeper into the hills. On the east side of the choppy belt the wagon had turned northeast, directly toward the settlements about Prairie City. Jim's first rankled impulse was to follow on to find out for sure where the beef had been taken. Yet the very openness of the thieving was enough to make him hesitate. He turned back.

He cut straight across the bench, afterward coming to the lake road just short of Tack. When he reached Bill's house, there was no one there. But Jim hunted around until he found a piece of paper and the stub tend of a pencil.

He wrote a note: "Bill, somebody's rustling on you. I found butchering sign over in the chop hills, and a wagon took the meat to Prairie. Don't poke into that without seeing me first. It's got the earmarks of a deadfall."

He put the note in the coffee can, where no one else would see it, but where Bill would be sure to find it, then he headed on down the Dry toward home.

CHAPTER 10

BOILER SPRINGS WAS TACK'S MAIN WATER ON THE bench; an oblate, bottom-fed pond of some size, it stood in the shadow of Pilot Butte and was inclosed by a fence that permitted Bill Trevers to pen the different range bunches that came in to drink and brand the calves missed or too small for the iron during the regular spring roundup. The gate was closed now, although the first stars were out, and some thirty head of cows, many with calves, hung about outside the inclosure. Occasionally one of the thirsty beasts would move forward, nuzzle the gate uneasily, then turn back.

When Jim rode up to the spring he was puzzling as to what had happened. The obvious explanation was that Bill had closed the gate that morning when he made his regular rounds, intending to let the cattle collect outside and return later in the day to let them in and trap them so that, if there were any slick-ears, he could burn on his brand. Yet night had come and except in the unlikely event that Bill had forgotten all about it he would have at least returned by now to open the gate and let the animals in.

Jim was tempted to do that now for the day had been hot and the steers wanted water. Yet the purpose that had brought him forth made him hesitate. All day he had worried about the glaring rustling evidence he had come upon in the choppies, a double concern now that the beef roundup was near and so many ranchers would soon be away from home range for weeks. He had decided to post himself on Signal Butte, which gave a commanding view of much of Tack's local range, and see, what the starlight might show him.

He had a sudden feeling that it might not have been Bill who closed the gate. This natural way of bunching scattered cattle and holding them for a swift selection and pickup would appeal to a cattle thief. All at once his faint worry that something had happened to Bill to prevent his returning left Jim. He would still keep a lookout from the butte, with more hope than ever that he would see something revealing. He rode back to the west side of the mound, left his horse secured there, then began to climb on the blind side of the eminence to the top.

He lay stretched flat there, the whole sweep of the eastern distance revealed to him sufficiently to warn him in advance of approach. Roundup had a special meaning for him this year, he thought as he settled down patiently. Afterward, when the cattle were shipped, there was to be a big wedding on Tack to celebrate the uniting of two pioneer lake families. He would be invited, he would go; after the ceremony he would kiss the bride, offer the lucky man his congratulations, and never in a rugged life would he have done anything harder.

He wasn't sure why he had known from the start that the feeling Nora had for Peyt was unnatural, at least as the foundation of a successful marriage. He doubted that Peyt even sensed her deep capacity for a true, woman's response to a man, much less aroused it. On the other hand, every time they had been together Jim had sensed a lift in her, a change of which she was herself aware and which she fought, which was as unfair to her as it was to him. He had without compunction tried to take her away from Peyt, which event in the end would be the kindest outcome all around. That had failed, and he knew that he had to play the loser's role with all the grace he could manage, for once she had taken the final step he wanted her to have no doubts to carry with her.

Presently Jim saw, far out on the prairie, not the one rider he expected but two horsemen coming on toward him. They rode at an easy gait, so that it was some time before their shapes grew larger, clearer in the starshine. They had beyond doubt waited somewhere near until Bill had made his visit to the pond, afterward coming in to close the gate, meaning to return in the night hours to pick up some of the cattle held there by thirst. He now knew their method of working, the ready market for the fresh meat they had found in Prairie. He had his choice between breaking up this night's attempt, with luck capturing them, or of letting them go far enough for him to find out if there were more members of their gang. He

94

chose to watch awhile, for it would be of little value to stop this raid without preventing, if possible, further forays on bench beef, which lay so invitingly exposed to the nester colony.

They came in boldly on the spring, not expecting trouble because of the cattle gathered outside the fence. In below him, while they stopped to look over the gather, they gave him a curious feeling that he ought to recognize them. This had bothered him only a moment before he realized that from their sizes and mounts they reminded him of Quigley and Rankin, the survivors of the battle on the Red Butte. Although in the obscurity he could not tell for sure, this partial recognition sent an increased hostility through him. Al Vassey had literally shot their jobs from under them, so they had turned to making their money off lake country cattle.

Checking his churning feelings, Jim pondered whether they would be working alone or if they had gathered more of their disreputable kind to help them. It would be poor judgment to act hastily, and he fought off the urge to tangle on the spot. The riders began to work through the cattle, selecting what they wanted. In a moment they drove two steers off to a distance where one man remained with them while the other turned back. They made four more choices that way, taking the pick of the lot and moving them out. Afterward one man came back again, opened the gate to let the rest of the cattle in to water. The little stolen cut was gently hazed forward.

Working in this manner, they could not help leaving copious sign, and Jim doubted that they would return to Boiler Spring again, at least for some time, but would switch the operation to other water holes of which there were plenty. That accounted for their carelessness with sign, which had puzzled him that morning. It also made it advisable that he see where they took this cut, so, descending from the butte, he mounted his horse and rode around to the other side.

He had to let them get out of sight for they would be watching their back trail and could see him as plainly as he could see them. Presently, when there was nothing to guide him but the occasional bawl of a steer not wanting to leave its regular bunch, he struck out. The thieves continued steadily eastward to the Moccasin road, crossed it at approximately the same point as previously, and continued on. They apparently thought it safe to do the butchering at the same place one more time.

Convinced they were going back to the little lake in the chop hills, Jim immediately cut slantwise to the north and, when he deemed himself well out of earshot, he lifted his mount to a fast gallop. He reached the first belt of low hills about a mile above the point where he had entered before, found a place to cross there, then gradually came in on the lake from that direction, observing as he neared the little water body that there was no wagon waiting there. For a moment he thought from this that he had guessed wrong as to their butchering place this time, then it occurred to him that they were not yet ready to beef this new gather.

He sat his horse for several minutes figuring what he should do next. They had to be caught red-handed, and while they at present had stolen stock on their hands, he knew that luck would have to be with him for him to take them without help. Yet he wanted to try it before they changed their method and went to work somewhere else. Reflecting, he remembered that the little canyon between the shouldering hills, through which the previous bunch had been brought, was brushy and winding. After only a moment's hesitation he rode back across the open and entered the defile.

It was not long after he had stationed himself, still mounted, in a brush screen in the gulch at a point where it turned, that he heard them coming on. A man shouted boldly now that they were well away from any habitation, and he knew they were heading the steers into the opening. He had a gun in his hand.

Presently the first steer came around the turn, sensed as much as saw the partly hidden horse and swung about. Jim held the horse motionless and, as others crowded behind, the lead steer came on. Jim sat tensely, ready to rap out an order the instant the riders appeared, for they would be close enough for him to blast them from the saddle before they could resist. Yet a long moment passed without their appearance, then another, and finally he wondered if they had caught onto him somehow.

He waited five minutes more before he grew convinced that they were too wily for him. He dared not ride out through this same passage, perhaps into a trap of their setting, so he swung and rode the other way. Recrossing the hills the way he had come in a little before, he came again onto the open bench and could see nothing of the night riders. Hoping they were waiting in the passage for him to come on through, he rode quietly down toward it. They were not in evidence at the opening and he passed warily through the canyon from that side to find it empty. The steers had hurried on to the little lake, thirsty since they had been denied water back at Boiler Spring.

He began to wonder if the thieves had turned back for another gather somewhere else, assured that the water and grass here would hold this cut for a time. Whatever, he had grown aware of the folly of trying to cope with the situation alone and, riding out to the open prairie, he struck across it.

Nora was home, sitting on the porch in the starlight and finding herself at a loss to understand the feelings that had stirred in her against her will all day. She and Bill had brought Ellen to Tack that afternoon, at Peyt's insistence more than anyone else's wish, for Peyt had argued strongly that it was the best arrangement all around. With Ellen here, Nora could take care of her and her father as well, Bill would like it even if Ellen would prefer to stay in her own home, and it made it easier for his men to live on Five without the presence of women while they took care of it.

The feeling that she did not fully understand Peyt had come when she met him on the east end of the lake and he had stalled about canceling the option he held on Roman Five. It had not been put down when, that same evening, he had come to the Five to see her with the report that, in Prairie, Gallant had again threatened the ranch, especially Bill, so that it was advisable for Peyt to keep holding the option, with some of his own men there to protect the Five's open range. Somehow, when they left with Ellen in the buckboard, she had had the feeling of their being dispossessed, with Crown moving in, a thoroughly guilty feeling that made her ashamed of herself.

There had been times before when she had been made to realize the devious way in which Peyt could act, pressing for some end he kept hidden, for—living without many confidants—he had developed a natural secretiveness. Now she wondered how it could be that he had been so hesitant about such a deal with Ellen

98

only to become overly enthusiastic for it. She knew his counsel of letting things stand as they were for a while had disturbed Bill and Ellen as much as herself. Right now those two were sitting indoors together, happy in their own company, assured of that companionship in the future if only things worked out for them.

She held herself to blame for having conceived the idea and pressed it with Peyt, and finally she let herself do what she had been resisting—wonder if Jim had sensed danger in such an arrangement when, that time, he had tried to talk her out of suggesting it. At the moment she had put it down to the dislike she knew to exist between the two men—a feeling that had never flattered her though it was over her affections—yet it was bewildering and alarming to be made uneasy herself by Peyt for the first time in their lives. This did not lessen her affection for him a whit, all along she had considered him justified in being a strange, aloof person. The circumstances in which he had lived had made him that.

Nora grew aware of a horse coming along the Dry well before it and the rider broke out of the cottonwoods. It probably was Jim, and this disturbed her for he kept himself so busy they would not see him for days on end unless something special brought him. A little later she knew it was he, and she had moved down the steps into the yard by the time he rode in.

"More trouble, Jim?" she asked.

He swung down and, instead of answering her question, said, "When did you get home?"

"Dad and I brought Ellen over here today."

She heard his breath pull in as he stared at her, then he said, "Is Peyt taking over at Five?"

"He's having a couple of men move over there. He

saw Gallant the other day, and Gallant made threats. It's best all around." She hadn't been sure of that herself but had to make him think so. Yet he didn't think so, for he made an impatient motion of his hand.

"Where's Bill?" he asked.

"In with Ellen. I guess you haven't heard yet that they're going to be married."

"So Bill did it," Jim said, pleased. "Will they live there?"

She found herself averse to telling him just what the situation was. "I don't think that's decided yet," she said.

"Going to be a double wedding?"

The idea startled, then pleased her. "I hadn't thought of it, but wouldn't it be nice? I'm going to suggest it."

"I kind of wanted to see Bill alone. Would you send him out?"

That confirmed her first fear, and she said, "I'm not the fragile kind of woman, Jim. You know that. Something's wrong, and I want to know what it is."

"Didn't Bill get the note I left in the coffee can about rustlers?"

"Why, we haven't made coffee since we got home," she said. "Rustlers, Jim? Where?"

"They've taken two small lifts off Tack that I know of, maybe more someplace else. They moved a little cut into the choppies tonight and vanished, maybe to pick up another. I thought I ought to have help."

Nodding, Nora turned and went into the house, a moment later coming out with her father. Jim explained what he had seen that morning and again that night.

Bill swore out loud. "Fine time for rustling to break out. What do you think we ought to do?"

"It might be foolish to jump in with both feet," Jim

100

said. "We don't know enough about what they're doing. We've got to do a thorough job or we won't do much good. They might not try Boiler Spring again or use the same hide-out, but they'll keep working on the bench for it's the handiest. Mainly I wanted to make sure you don't blunder into them or get riled and go after them by yourself. They'll likely keep working the fenced water holes and moving the stuff someplace in the hills. That'll give us a chance to set a trap. I'll see you tomorrow evening."

"Meanwhile I'll keep my eyes open."

"And congratulations, Bill. You and Peyt are getting the world's finest women, and I think you've got the sense to know it."

"That was a left-handed remark," Nora said hotly. "I suppose Peyt hasn't."

"I wish he had," Jim answered. "Good night." He rode out.

CHAPTER 11

As he had breakfast with Ellen and Nora, Bill Trevers was so pleased, made so happy by the change in his life, that all his troubles seemed easy to overcome, all his desires so sure of fulfillment. A spare man, he ate sparingly yet with relish, and whenever he caught Ellen's eye he saw there the old lively vitality that had made her so appealing to him as a young woman. He realized that this came from something within that had never aged and never could, something that was more than her own happiness and hope, that it involved also a genuine affection for him. For this reason he was quite positive that he and Jim would soon have the rustling cleaned up, even that Nora would find this same happiness with Peyt.

Delighted by what she saw in her father and the woman who would soon give her a real mother again, Nora rose from the table as Bill did, looked about the kitchen with some uncertainty, then took the teakettle out to the pump to fill it. Ellen smiled at the stratagem, and thus emboldened, Bill bent down and kissed her. The pleasure that coursed in him in result made him think, I'm not an old man, not entirely.

"Be back for dinner, Bill," she said gently.

"Let anybody try to keep me away," he said, and found his hat and went out.

At the pump as he passed Nora said, "You'll be careful now, won't you?"

"Tell me something." Bill returned. "Does Peyt make you want to whoop and holler like I want to?"

"Why, what a question," she gasped.

He grinned and went on to the horse corral. When he had roped and saddled a horse he went astride and rode out. The morning's heat was building already but he was so used to it he scarcely noticed. He rode down the Dry for a distance, then took the well-worn cattle and horse trail that led to the notch in the bluffs. He made the short, easy climb to the table and saw before him the great wheeling bench he had claimed so long ago, that he knew so well.

It was hard to estimate how many times he had done this daily trouble riding, alert for and taking care of the scores of little things that could go wrong, sometimes encountering a big trouble. He guessed there was no more independent, satisfying a life than a cowman's, yet it had been so much more so in the old days, when all this country was wild and challenging, when the forces

102

of life had moved more vigorously in himself.

He wasn't sure, though, that he envied the young people, for whom life still ran as limitless and inviting as all this prairie. What they gained in freshness of passion and pleasure they lost in the mellowness that came only with the years, some hard, some easy, all contributing. He had known hunger and joy in the winning and having of Lucy, sorrow and loneliness in the loss of her, and then he had known the long years in that twilight zone of middle age when lost laughter was still regretted, coming finally to this fullness, this climax in the long transition of Bill Trevers.

He saw cattle spread out from him presently, his cattle, and here and there an old retired cow horse that out of gratitude he had put on a pension of grass. Each of the mounts had a memory attached, and right now he was looking out fondly toward old Pike, who, as a colt, had carried him on a reckless night ride to Moccasin when Nora came into the world. He had killed another horse, whose presence he somehow sensed this morning on this very range, the day several years later when, arriving in Moccasin to find the doctor away, he had ridden on the old Crow Track, forty miles east, where the doctor had been called. It had been too late when they got back—Lucy and his little son, half born, were both gone.

There was tranquility everywhere this morning, nothing to hold him up. He visited the artificial tank he had built in a draw on his north line, adjoining the big Crown, riding the line thereafter to throw back any strays that might have moved across. The line, which existed only in the minds of men, running from landmark to landmark, might have been a fence for nothing had breached it. When he reached Indian Well he turned south toward Boiler Spring, now looking for evidence of bunched cattle, driven by thieves, and finding none.

The gate at Boiler was open as it should be, he saw when he came in on the east side of the butte, a couple of steers drinking, a few others lying down outside, showing they had already filled up. Bill rode to the fence, eased his seat in the saddle, and pulled out his pipe and loaded it. When he had lighted up and enjoyed a few puffs, he swung the horse and moved on. The pen had a Texas gate of barbed wire that could be drawn across the opening, and as he reached it he saw plainly the imprint on the soft sandy soil of boots too large to be his own, and he wondered how he had happened to miss them before.

He was not uneasy now for it seemed probable, as Jim had, believed, that the thieves would not crowd their luck by working the same water more than a time or two. Assured that everything was in order here, he rode toward the south end of the butte to pass around and start in toward the Dry. It was rocky at the butte's south end, and in this morning hour the upthrusts threw black shadows on the yellow ground. He passed into the field, then with no warning at all a sudden fear jerked across him as a voice rang out.

"Hold up there, old-timer."

Bill threw a startled look to his right. A man stood there and held a pistol that was pointed at the thick of Bill's body. He needed shaving, his clothes were grimy, but the hard eyes were all that existed for Bill in the magnification projected by his alarm.

"What's this?" he managed to gasp.

The man said, "Don't move," and started forward. As he neared, Bill saw how closely he fitted the description Jim had given of the two Gallant men who had survived the Red Butte fight, the men he thought he had recognized with the stolen cattle the night before, this where you lived a good part of your life."

"Tack's just across the lake from it."

"Ellen," he thundered, "marry me now so we can tackle the thing together. I'm going to tell Nora and have her get that option back from Peyt. I'm going to fetch out a preacher to team us up. Before bad weather I'm taking you to Hot Springs. And I don't want any more argument against it."

Her eyes were shining, the dark-rimmed eyes were full of life again as she recoiled then lifted to his intense feeling. "You really mean it," she breathed. "You really want it. Peyt's check is in that drawer there, Bill. Nora will want to give it back to him."

"You'll do it?" he cried.

"Yes, Bill—oh, yes."

Bill found the check and went thumping out of the house. He saw Nora down by the lake, sitting with her back against a tree. He was happier than he had been in years as he hurried down the gentle slope and joined her.

Breathlessly he said, "I've got good news. Ellen just promised to marry me.

"Marry you?" she gasped.

"And what's wrong with that?"

The surprise left her face, and all at once she laughed delightedly. "Why, nothing. It's wonderful for both of you. But what will you do—go with her?"

"I'm sending her to Hot Springs to get well. Then she'll come back. She told me about the deal with Peyt. I want you to get her out of that because I'm going to live on the Five and run it. It's been her home too long for her to give it up. A woman's more that way than a man, and Tack don't mean that much to me. Jim wants to take it over, buy it in time."

"How do you know he does?"

84

being the larger of that pair. That made him Rankin, and Quigley was probably somewhere near, staying with the horses at enough distance the animals would not tip off the waylay.

"I said what's this?" Bill repeated.

The man reached up and took the gun from Bill's holster; he stepped back. Without moving his eyes off Bill, he shouted, "I got him, Milt, come on!"

Bill felt sweat run down his sides. His first thought was that he had caught them shutting the spring gate for another cattle steal, but that did not explain this. They had hidden themselves well, he hadn't been suspicious, and they could simply have let him pass on. They had wanted him, that was why they were here this early, and he didn't like the look of it.

In a moment a rider came in from the west side of the butte, leading a second horse. His appearance convinced Bill that they were the men Jim believed them to be. Gallant men, at least indirectly, and Bill tried to figure it out.

The big man swung up, tipped a nod to the east, and said, "All right, old man, get going."

"Now you look here," Bill retorted. "I know you two. Rankin and Quigley that tried to help Morgan homestead on the Red Butte. Gallant was behind Morgan, and he must still be behind you. What's the idea of this, anyhow?"

Quigley looked uneasy and, noting that, Rankin said, "It, don't matter if he knows who we are, Milt. He ain't going to talk."

"I guess it don't," Quigley said, and shrugged. "Trevers, he said for you to get riding."

"So you know my name, whose cattle you've been stealing."

"Not that we intended to send you the money,

105

Trevers," Rankin said, and laughed. "You better lead his horse, Milt. I'll follow."

Bill knew by then that they meant business, that resistance would be as disastrous as whatever lay ahead. Quigley led the way out of the rock field and struck out across the open prairie. Far forward nearly hazed from view in the distance, lay the chop hills where Jim said they had been taking the cattle. He knew they were going there, all that puzzled him was what for.

The cattle thieves kept a close watch on the vast roundabout as they rode, and Bill saw from the copious evidence underfoot that they were taking their usual route. On and on, the brassy fat sun due ahead, the prairie's stillness broken only by the creak of leather and the scuffing sound of hoofs, varied only now and then when Quigley hawked and spat. Before they came to the Moccasin road the two gave a careful look in either direction, Bill unable to resist doing the same but out of hope rather than fear that someone might be coming along. But Moccasin was a dead town now, only a few went there, and he saw nothing but the empty road sinuously twisting across the prairie. The little horseback party cut the road and not long afterward entered the canyon into the hills.

It was as Jim had described it, Bill found. They passed the brush clump in the canyon where Jim must have waited, hoping to surprise this pair, they emerged presently into a narrow, ridge-bound little valley with a tree-fringed pond in its center. Again there was no wagon there, but Bill saw at once the six Tack steers they had brought in after dark the previous evening. Quigley rode directly to the big tree with the limb showing rope marks and halted. He swiveled in the saddle and looked back.

"How long we going to wait?" he called.

"Long enough to see if anybody's following. Get down, Trevers."

Bill swung out of the saddle. The other two dismounted, and Quigley took all three horses farther down the lake and tied them. When he came back he said, "Should have fetched a rope. I think we ought to tie him up."

"We don't want any marks on him."

"If you don't mind," Bill said, "I'd like to know what you're up to."

What Rankin said about wondering who might be following suggested that they were aware of Jim's trailing them the previous night, which seemed reasonable since they had faded out instead of falling into his trap. The person most apt to discover rustling sign at Boiler would be its owner, so maybe they thought he had laid for them there, followed them here, and wanted to know what steps had been taken to spoil their game. Yet why couldn't they have tried to find that out at the spring?

Rankin stared at Bill as if considering his question, then said, "You might as well set down, Trevers. It'll be a while."

Bill seated himself with his back to a tree. Quigley sank down at a safe distance and sat cross-legged like an Indian, his small, opaque eyes staring at Bill. Rankin moved down to the water, flattened, and drank. After he straightened he sat there, rolling a cigarette. Bill wished now he hadn't charged them with stealing his cattle; if he had played ignorant, they might not have felt impelled to bring him here.

His hope now was that they would remain here long enough for Nora to grow uneasy, which she would since he had promised Ellen to be in at noon, and she had heard what Jim said the night before about rustling. Jim would know where to look if she could get hold of him, which she would try to do if he still had not come home by midafternoon, a matter of another four or five hours. Then he knew dismally that she would not be able to find Jim, who would be off somewhere at work. She might not see him until, as he had promised, he came to Tack in the evening.

After what seemed an hour to Bill, Rankin shoved to a stand, brushed the sand from his pants, then, wordlessly, walked down to the horses. Mounted, he rode out toward the canyon, entered it, and disappeared. Bill looked back at Quigley, who didn't seem to have removed those beady eyes from him once. He didn't even seem to blink.

Bill had no desire to smoke, but when the footfalls of Rankin's horse had faded he pulled out his pipe, tested it by blowing on the stem. Shaking his head, he reached into his pocket for his jackknife as if to ream the bowl, but Quigley rapped, "None of that. Stand up, old man, and let's see what you've got in that pocket." Bill rose stiffly to his feet and Quigley came in warily. He patted Bill's pocket and said, "A toad-stabber, is it? I'll take that."

"You going to get it?" Bill said. "Or me?"

"Hand it over."

Bill fished out the knife and held it forth to Quigley, who had stepped back, hoping he would reach a hand for it.

"Toss it," Quigley said.

Bill did. "Rankin seems to be the big chief," he said. "And about as gabby as an Indian, too."

"Never mind that."

Bill put his pipe into his teeth, blew it open, then reached for his tobacco. He opened the drawstring of the red sack with his left hand, and when it was fully open

108

he swung his right, flinging the loosened tobacco full into Quigley's eyes. The man yelped, lifted his hands protectively, and Bill punched him hard in the belly. As, gagging and bent, Quigley staggered back, Bill made a grab for the man's gun, but Quigley caught his wrist. The only thing Bill could do then was close with him, using his head to butt the man's face, then by wrenching and swinging violently Quigley threw him off balance and they went down in a crash.

Bill rolled desperately, his age and stiff joints as great a drawback as his natural stringiness, considering the youth and size of this man. He managed to turn Quigley under him, the only sound their breathing and grunting; he freed an arm and his fist pounded the fellow's sweating, twisted face. Quigley cursed him, then knocked him off, but Bill managed to grab him again before he could pull his gun.

"Cut it out!" Quigley panted then. "I don't want to beat you up!"

Bill's answer was to ram his head against Quigley's mouth. Again and again he jarred the man, knocking his head back, keeping him helpless. But he was playing out, and all at once Quigley drew up his legs, gave them a mighty thrust that threw Bill off. Quigley scrambled to his feet. He got his gun gripped in his hand at last.

"I can kill you, Trevers!" he panted. "We just don't want you to look beat up! Stay still or you get it right now."

Disdainfully Bill pushed himself to a dazed, sick, sitting position, staring at the fellow with half-seeing eyes, dimly aware that this thing surpassed his worst fears. Quigley's mouth was bleeding and the blood mixed with sweat on his chin. His gimlet eyes were puffing, they spat a vicious antipathy. Bill dragged himself over under the tree, propped his back against the trunk, and sat sucking in noisy breaths while his head cleared. He was helpless in physical terms, the only thing he could do was try a bluff when Rankin got back.

The man was a long while in coming. Then Rankin appeared in the canyon mouth and rode forward toward the lake. As he drew up he looked at Quigley, then Bill, and said, "What the hell?"

"The old boy got rambunctious," Quigley said waspishly. "But I never marked him up. I let him do this to me to keep from it. You see anything out there?"

Rankin shook his head and swung down.

"Now just a minute," Bill said. "Maybe you didn't see anything, but you don't know everything, either. One thing is that a man was on your trail last night and knows who you are, what you've been up to. Otherwise how'd I recognize you except from his description? I never seen you before. I wasn't up the Red Butte the morning you come out with the sheriff for the inquest. Think twice before you do anything that'll get you in worse trouble."

Rankin looked at Quigley and said, "He means that Carlin. But nobody was on our trail last night, Trevers."

"You can go up that canyon a ways," Bill retorted, "and find horse tracks back of some bushes where he waited for you. Go and see."

"I sure will," Rankin said, and swung back on his horse.

He rode into the canyon, was gone ten minutes, then he came back.

"There's tracks there, all right," he told Quigley, "and it must have been Carlin. We better wait awhile longer."

110

CHAPTER 12

HE HAD VISITED THREE FENCED WATER HOLES ON HIS own range without finding a shut gate, which would be proof that the night held trouble. When he came to the last one Jim swung down, built a smoke, and rested. He was out much later than usual, dusk had run in, and he knew he would have a late supper that night since an hour's riding lay between him and home, and afterward he had to go up to see Bill.

He had decided that the rustlers would not pick more beef off the grass until the steers hidden in the chop hills had been butchered and disposed of, so there was no hurry. At none of the places he had visited had he seen evidence of strangers looking things over, and he wondered if, instead, they would now turn their attention to Crown range, which lay as handy to Prairie but which was more carefully watched by Peyt's big crew. He wouldn't worry about Crown, which was able to look out for itself. Bill had a water hole at Indian Well and a dirt tank closer to headquarters, and tomorrow, Jim decided, he would keep an eye on them.

When he had finished his smoke he stepped up and rode north, still not hurrying for his loss of sleep the night before caught up with him and he let the horse pick its own way while he drowsed in the saddle. He was riding into his own yard before he came fully awake, and when he had put up the horse and pumped water into the trough he wished he could go to bed without having to make the long ride to Tack.

He came finally into his kitchen, and the moment he struck a match he saw a paper on the table, propped against the lamp to attract his attention. Thinking it was a message from Bill, he hastily lighted the lamp and tilted the note to the light, at once seeing a woman's writing and Nora's name at the end.

"Jim, it's nearly four o'clock and Dad hasn't been home all day. He was to be back at noon. I'll go home by way of Boiler Spring. Come as soon as you can."

Jim stared at the paper a long moment. It was an hour after dark, which meant that Nora had left it there some six hours before. He blew out the lamp and hurried back to the corral, his fatigue and hunger forgotten in the sudden urgency pushing him. He had meant to catch a fresh horse, now there wasn't time, and the one he had just turned in still stood at the water trough. In a few minutes he was riding north.

He was tempted at first to go by Boiler himself. But there was a chance that by now Nora and Bill were both back home, with some explanation less frightening than the one haunting the back of his mind for Bill's long absence. Therefore he took the trail up the narrows, riding fast now that the stars were bright and numerous, letting him see the under-footing.

The sound of his arriving at Tack brought Nora into the yard alone. She cried, "Jim! I was afraid you'd got into trouble, too!"

He swung down beside her. "No news from Bill?"

"He hasn't come home. I came by Boiler, but there was no sign of him there. I didn't go on to Indian Well, thinking he might be back here or you'd be coming pretty soon."

"I was out longer than usual," he said bitterly. "Did Bill take a rifle when he left?"

"Just his side gun. The last thing he said was that he'd be careful. He told Ellen he'd be in at noon sure. Oh, Jim—what's happened?"

112

"I'll stop at the tank and go on to Indian," he decided quickly. "Try not to worry. Maybe he just lost his horse."

"He's had time to walk in from anywhere on our range," she said dismally. "Something's happened to him, Jim. I know it."

He put a hand on her arm, then turned and rose again to the saddle.

"Find him, Jim," she whispered.

"I won't be back till I do."

He rode at a rushing speed as he passed back along the creek, turned in to the bluffs, and climbed to the table. He was not as familiar with Tack's range as with his own, and at this hour distances and landmarks took on an eerie distortion confusing to the most experienced rangemen. Thus he missed Bill's dirt tank the first try, cutting too far north, then having to pick his way carefully until he found the draw that held it. Several steers were resting about the tank; they rose and ambled off as he came in.

There was nothing else there to help Jim. This water was not fenced, yet a thief could wait and pick up cattle as thirst brought them in, and he had to be thorough. He looked around very carefully, then rode on, moving up to what he believed to be the Crown lower line, then heading east, which course would take him to Indian Well, another spring that, like Boiler, was inclosed to help work the cattle.

He drove his jaded horse hard, but even then they seemed barely to crawl. Once he lost precious time when he discerned in the distance some low shape on the ground off to his right. He investigated, finding a young cow trying to calve, down already from some difficulty. There was no time to help, and he went on.

The gate was open at the outermost spring. Bill was not there, had left no sign of having been there although now Jim scouted the adjoining area with care. Disappointed again, he sat a moment wondering if he should ride on north to Crown, report the whole trouble, and start an organized search. But that would take time, Bill might need help this very minute, and Jim decided to have his own look at Boiler, although in the night it would be hard to find anything Nora might have missed that afternoon. He reached Bill's last water hole some two hours after leaving Tack. Frustration rose hard against his drive as he came in and swung down. This place was as serene, undisturbed as the others. From here Bill would have ridden back to the Dry and followed it home. Nora would have gone in that way, too, would have come upon him if some accident, such as a horse falling and pinning him, had occurred along there.

Here was where the rustlers had twice picked up cattle. It seemed out of the question to Jim that Bill, after reaching here on his daily rounds, had let temper take him over into the chop hills so he could bring back his steers. There was nothing foolish about Bill Trevers and, besides, he had agreed to the wisdom of their working together, slowly and carefully so as to make sure of results. The only thing left was to follow in to the Dry and back to Tack—somehow he knew already that it would be unrewarding—and tell Nora they would have to wait for daylight, when a bigger search could be started, with light to see more sign.

All at once a strange thought entered his mind, previously blocked by its unlikeliness. Some new development might have taken Bill into the lake hideout, where he had run into trouble. Jim knew it would take him a couple of hours out of his way, but it was worth riding in there to see what he could uncover. He struck out across the open prairie.

Until he came to the hills he rode in a direct rush. He knew there was every chance that the regular entrance to the choppy-locked lake was under guard now, so he went slantwise toward the rougher, more northerly entrance he had used the evening before. Reaching the hugging stricture, he slowed his horse to a quiet walk, riding alertly, not sure but what he might encounter trouble even here. When he reached the far end he halted through several breaths while his ears keened the night. He heard nothing but the soft sound of breeze on the sandy ridges and, after a moment of this, he rode south, hugging a hill where his shape was blended into a darker background.

Much closer to the lake he saw the Tack steers bedded down, proving that no disturbance had caused the rustlers to move them out of here. Then he saw, well south of the lake, the shape of a grazing horse. He pulled down, staring at it, his eyes focusing sharply until he was sure of his impression that it was saddled. He decided at once that it belonged to a sentry in the canyon, and the discovery pulled his shoulders tight with tension. It was an opportunity to take one of them into custody by slipping up unexpectedly from this side, and he pondered the wisdom of this. He decided against it; the capture of one would only scare the other away.

He cut directly across and into the trees at the edge of the lake. Better concealed, he moved on down the shore toward the big tree where they had butchered. Then all at once he pulled up his horse and grabbed for his gun. A man lay there by the tree as if asleep. That was the sentry since there was only one saddle horse, and he wasn't in the canyon but here, soldiering. Jim swung down lightly, trailed reins, and slipped on afoot.

All at once a staggering jar went through his nervous system, and he yelled, "Bill—Bill!"

He ran forward, dropping to his knees, knowing already he was too late. One starlit glimpse of Bill's head was enough to tell him that no one could help Bill now.

For moments Jim knelt there, fighting to clear the numbness from his brain, to understand how a thing so unpredictable, so brutal, could have happened. He knew now that no one else was here, that for some reason Bill had come to this forbidden area and run into death. Rankin—Quigley—he thought in benumbed bitterness. He wondered why they hadn't dumped Bill's weighted body in the lake as callously as they had murdered him, running off his horse, covering this up. Panic, maybe. They had cause. Whether or not they realized it, someone knew they had done this thing and would call them to account. Or maybe they had wanted him to be found.

Jim took out his bandana and laid it gently over Bill's face. He went back to his horse, mounted, and rode down to where the other horse grazed, dragging its reins. It was Bill's, as he now expected. Maybe Bill had ridden in to the tree, seen where the beef carcasses had been hoisted for butchering, and been caught there. Jim got the reins and led the horse back.

He knew the body should be left here for the sheriff, but he couldn't stay, nor could he leave it for molestation by varmints. It was cool, stiffened, but he managed to lash it to the saddle of the led horse. He rode out boldly through the main canyon, hoping they would jump him. But nothing happened. Presently he was making a much slower ride of it across the prairie, back to Tack, taking Bill Trevers home.

He tried to come into Tack quietly, in the last starlight before dawn, but Nora was on the porch waiting and saw him and came running and crying out. Jim swung down quickly and hurried toward her, catching her at the sides, holding her tight.

"Easy, girl—easy."

He felt her tremble, he felt a sob tear up in her before he heard it issued. Then she was limp, her face against his chest, and thus it happened to her, the impact, then the recovery. He felt the firming of her body, then, "Where was he?" she asked.

"At the hide-out. I don't know what took him there."

"Bring him in, please," she said.

"Is Ellen still up?"

"I tried to get her to sleep in a chair. I doubt that she did. Oh—Jim!"

He put his arms around her, very gently he kissed her hair. She cried then, which was better for her, then she turned and fled. He took Bill into the house, afterward, through the dark hallway and into his bedroom. He covered him up with a quilt.

The two women sat in the darkness when Jim walked across the hall into the main room of the house. He moved to the center table and lighted a lamp, almost wishing he hadn't when he saw their faces but knowing it was better for them. He looked at them.

"I'll go to Prairie," he said. "Do you want me to send Peyt over, Nora?"

"I don't care."

Nora rose then and went into the room with her father, and Jim decided to let her be there with the man she had loved so well. He looked into the face of Ellen

117

and saw marked anew what had been there the day Al was killed. Doubly stricken, two loved men gone.

He said, "I'm sorry. I can't tell you how much."

"He was happy this morning. I'm glad of that."

"I know who it was, Mrs. Vassey. The men who survived at the Red Butte and killed Al. The same pair—Gallant hirelings."

Ellen looked at him in pained bewilderment. "But why Bill? Nora won't have to sell Tack, she's going to marry Peyt next month."

"So she is," Jim said and that was all. For the first time it came to him that Ellen was back where she was before Bill asked her to become his wife. The thing began to make sense at last.

Reaction hit him then, and he felt spent, ready to drop himself. Going into the kitchen, he started a fire. There was coffee in the big pot and he pulled it forward to heat. Lighting a lamp there, he sat down at the kitchen table. He rolled a cigarette absently, not tasting its flavor after he had lighted it.

Rustling, he knew now with sure clarity, had not been Rankin's and Quigley's main purpose in their activities on the bench, which accounted for their carelessness with evidence. Probably they had hoped to draw Bill into a trap where he could be murdered, with it looking like the work of cattle thieves. That proving too slow, they must have laid in waiting for him at Pilot Butte, then taken him in and left him there, dead.

Ellen wheeled her chair into the kitchen just as Jim was pouring himself a cup of lukewarm coffee. She said, "I see what you mean, Jim. Gallant's still after the Five, not Tack, even after Peyt told him he holds an option on it."

The coffee sloshed in the cup in Jim's hand. "Peyt's

118

got an option on Five?" he asked.

"Didn't you know? I thought Nora or Bill had told you."

"I didn't know," Jim said. "Except that Nora thought it would be a good idea to have Peyt buy it to keep it out of Gallant's hands. I thought that was knocked in the head when you decided to marry Bill."

"I gave Peyt the option before Bill asked me."

"Peyt sure didn't lose any time."

"It was only kindness on his part. And I'll have to let him have the ranch now." Then, as if wanting to change a painful subject, she added quickly, "Don't you want something to eat, Jim?"

He shook his head. The rest of the coffee was getting hot at last, and he refilled his cup. When he had drunk it he went outdoors.

He used his own horse long enough to ride into the horse pasture and rope a fresh mount. Bringing it into the corral, he threw on a dry blanket, then changed his own saddle to its back. He led the horse up to the house, opened the kitchen door long enough to say, "I'm going to Prairie now," then he went up and rode east.

When he came to the lake shore, following the road to Crown, he paused, swinging his horse about, staring back at the Dry gap, picturing as he had once before the cheap, easily built earth dam that would impound a fortune in water. The thought was fixed in his mind now that Peyt's owning Five or Gallant's owning it might amount to the same thing. Bill was gone, Nora was soon to marry Peyt and was more easily influenced by him than Bill had been. It was an appalling thought but one he could not dislodge. Something very smooth and very deadly had been going on all along, the thing had not run its course, and there was probably worse to come.

119

He thought of Rye and Martha Jones, of Burt Tantro and his family, of the Sandses and Fred Downey—finally of himself. If Peyt retained his lifelong hold on Nora's mind, it would be very bad for them all.

He was going to Prairie now to telegraph for the sheriff, knowing that Landorf would see in the situation what the killers had worked hard to make him see. Whether or not he was persuaded, he would know the futility of trying to make more of it. There was only Jim Carlin to swear who had been both thieves and killers, a fact of which he believed Rankin and Quigley to be in ignorance. But they could blast his testimony in a minute; it was easy for their kind to establish an alibi.

His bitterness compounded with his grief for Bill Trevers, and his mouth ruled straight and hard as he rode on toward the new railroad town.

CHAPTER 13

DAWN OVER PRAIRIE WAS A SUDDEN BRILLIANCE, bringing out of the hot night the development about it on which rested its hopes, the floor of flat, sterile earth on which stood half a hundred tents, each on a portion of the tract Gallant was now optioning at a brisk pace. At dawn there was little more than the abodes in evidence, tents graying from the eternal dust, the empty streets of the town itself lined by establishments as artificially overgrown as the plans in the minds of their owners.

Gallant awakened from uneasy sleep to face another hot day, dreading it, not only because of the prairie's austerity—naturally unpleasant to a man of his tastes—but because each day seemed to produce a tightening of the situation in which he was caught. His sleep had not been good for a long while, and though part of this wakefulness was typical of middle age it had a direct cause in the fact that his ready cash—on which there was every kind of drain—was about exhausted.

He slid out of bed, padded in his nightshirt to the stand where he washed, scrubbed his teeth, then shaved. When he had dressed and completed his grooming by combing his thin hair, he looked better but felt the same as before. The hotel dining room was not ready to serve breakfast, none of the eating places on the street would be open yet, but often when the night had not passed well for him he took a walk along the strung-out street, then returned to his office. He now had special reason to want to be at his place of business early. A couple of men had promised him good news this morning, and if it came things could really start to boom. His was strictly the boom type of mind, there was no natural patience in it. It was also an astute mind, equipped with a gambler's sharp sense of empathy.

He was more keenly aware than ever of the enormous pressure in Prairie, which was increased each time Sam Weems sold a settler a dry tract and a paper promise. Gallant knew, as Weems did, that unless tangible evidence of a ditch from Silver Lake was produced shortly things would get out of hand, that if this happened he could control the situation no longer. He would try, as he and Weems were presently trying, to direct this force at the lake country, but he knew quite well that it could destroy him at the same time.

Stepping onto the street, Gallant again remarked the intense brightness of prairie light in summer, so much more evident as it clapped in to destroy the darkness each morning. Odors from the town and from the railroad track, the siding with its emigrant cars and the litter behind the buildings, seemed pooled, unstirred all night by human activity, and they were especially offensive to him. Pulling out a cigar, he bit off its tip and spat it out, then lighted the weed with the naptha taper that came aflame when dragged down the roughened side of its container. He took a couple of experimental puffs, clamped the cigar in his teeth, and turned east along the north side of the tracks.

When he had walked one side of the long street he returned on the other, climbed the stairs, and let himself into his office. Impounded heat and scent engulfed him and he went at once from window to window, throwing them open. A film of prairie dust had gathered on everything overnight, as it always did, but his clerks would clean the place when they came in, and he went to his desk and sat down, settling his feet on a pulled-out drawer for comfort.

When he heard a horse coming along the street he rose and went to the window. It was not one of the men he expected, but Jim Carlin. Gallant felt his shoulders jerk back as he stared down into the street, but Carlin didn't look up at him. Gallant waited there, seeing the Dry Creek rancher stop at the railroad depot and go in. He was out in a few minutes and looked both ways along Prairie's street, then he walked away and remounted. Gallant saw with relief that he was going the other way up the main street, but the relief was not great because he wondered uneasily whether this visit by Carlin was a good sign or bad. He had never forgotten what had happened to Honey Lagg and here in the office afterward.

With the street again empty and less threatening, Gallant found himself still drawn by the sight he had so often seen from this window, the imagined view of illusory emptiness, of a return to the primeval prairie, and he was again aware that his sense of his own impermanence rested upon the ephemerality of his works. There was in him for a moment a nagging regret that his life course, set long ago, carried him rushing on whether or not he would linger. He was going back to nature in the end himself as Prairie would, and often of late he had a disturbing feeling that it might be sooner than he figured.

Because he had lost track of Carlin he was startled when boots hit the stairs, coming up. He swung around and reseated himself at his desk, upright in the chair now, the center drawer of the desk pulled out slightly because of the gun that lay handily in there. He watched the outer door through the open inner door to the clerk's office. He had not relocked it, and when the door sprang open he was relieved to see Rankin come through, followed by Quigley.

The pair looked rougher, dirtier than ever, and now they also looked tired. Yet satisfaction marked their faces, they were proud of themselves this morning, and he knew the news was good.

"It's done," Rankin said, "and we want our money."

"You're sure it's done?"

"Damned sure. We've got a thousand coming. Cash."

"You seem to be in a hurry," Gallant reflected.

"You're damned right. That Carlin caught onto us."

Gallant felt as if someone had driven a knife into his back. He stared hard at Rankin, seeing less fear there than hurry. But Rankin didn't know what Gallant did.

"You damned fools," Gallant said bitterly. "Did you come straight to my office?"

"Hell, no," Rankin retorted. "We been at our hotel since about three this morning, waiting for you to show up. Seen you go up the street from our window." The man laughed. "You ordered it done, Gallant. What makes you so edgy?"

"Carlin's here. He went to the depot a while ago. I don't think he's left."

It was Rankin's turn to lose his composure. His mouth opened, and Quigley, who was rolling a cigarette, spilled tobacco.

"Are you sure he's wise?" Gallant pressed.

"No doubt of it," Rankin answered. "Old Trevers said Carlin trailed us into the hills with the first beef we took from that spring."

"And you went ahead and killed Trevers?" Gallant said furiously.

"That's what you ordered, Gallant. Get him, and the how was up to us. We got him. And if you're that scared it's apt to cost you more. In cash. Come on, man, pay us."

"I'll pay you," Gallant said, "and you've got to get, out of this country."

"That rustling setup's pretty good. Them steers are waiting like daisies to be picked. Me and Milt figure we've got a good thing."

"No more of that!" Gallant said savagely.

"All right. For two thousand we give it up and head for yonder."

Gallant went to his safe and opened it; he counted out the money. He made it the two thousand, resenting the pressure but knowing these men had to slip out of Prairie, never to return, or he was bound to become implicated with the killing of Trevers. The men divided the money and stowed it away.

"Go down the back stairs," Gallant said. "Don't let Carlin see you leave here."

"Who's afraid of him?" Quigley asked.

124

"I am, and if you knew him better you'd be. He knows about Trevers. He was filing a telegram to the sheriff at the depot. He knows you hang around here. So, damn you, be careful."

He watched them tramp down through the outer office then leave by the hall door. His palms and armpits were soaked with sweat. Carlin must be waiting for the sheriff, intending to take him out to the lake country. The man was incredible. Yet Gallant saw no way he could be tied in with the killers. All manner of men came to his office and at all hours. There was no apparent motive other than rustling for the killing, an occupational hazard of the cattle ranges.

A bright anger rose in Gallant with the feeling that he was a cat's-paw where he liked to enslave his own. Actually he had no assurance from Peyt Peyton that a right-of-way would be forthcoming when Peyt had acquired the land he wanted.

Peyt had never suggested anything dangerous to himself, had never said he wanted Vassey and Trevers killed, had only made his subtle suggestions and held up attractive bait. Gallant had made his guesses, taken the risks, and might only have lent himself to a design that would benefit him none at all.

Abruptly a voice rang out on the quiet street below him.

"Rankin!"

Gallant slung to the window, knowing that voice, having heard it here in this office. He saw Carlin on the other sidewalk. Rankin and Quigley were turning the corner ahead of him, making for their hotel down the ragged side street, past the livery barn. They hauled around as Gallant silently cursed them for their heedlessness. Had Carlin seen them coming down from

125

his office? A dryness hit Gallant's mouth as he watched, fascinated.

"Citizen's arrest!" Carlin shouted at the pair. "For murder!"

"The hell you say!" Rankin yelled, and reached for his gun.

He died on his feet. The crash of two guns split the morning, Rankin's driving its bullet into the sidewalk ahead of Carlin. Quigley swung and bolted toward the livery, whose doors now stood open. He made it, cutting from side to side as Carlin shot again. From the darkness of the barn aisle Quigley fired two hasty shots in retaliation. Carlin ran forward and was out of line with the doors. He crossed over the side street to the other walk, then moved on along the front wall of the big red barn.

Gallant knew that barn, where he rented a rig when forced to travel on the prairie. Set up for the farm trade, it had no corral for saddle horses, only stalls with mangers for the grangers' teams. Quigley wanted a riding horse, which he could not take out any way except through the front for the back door was high, giving onto a growing manure pile below it. Maybe Carlin knew that arrangement, too, for when he had edged a few paces along the barn wall he stopped. To Gallant he looked supremely cool and unruffled, as if this moment afforded him an extreme satisfaction. Across the vacant lot at the depot the telegrapher was staring through the wide window, like Gallant not in the line of fire and hypnotized by the violence of the moment.

Suddenly Carlin tensed as if listening. Then to Gallant's surprise he slid sleekly forward and disappeared into the barn. The expected shot did not crash out. Gallant sucked in slow shallow breaths,

126

staring. After a moment he saw Quigley carefully prowl forward along the outside of the barn. He had realized his predicament and chosen to go out over the manure pile. He had his gun in his grip and with each step he put his foot down slowly. He came to the corner of the barn and there waited. Gallant's own overwrought nerves tightened sympathetically. Then Quigley sprang around the corner.

His astonishment was manifest in the way he hauled up, staring blankly at the empty walk before him. He hung there hesitantly, seemed undecided whether to pull back or wait. He waited, his quarry lost to him, with no idea where Carlin had gone. Gallant wanted to shout to him but, even if he had deemed it wise, he could not have found his voice just then. Quigley cut a quick look at Rankin's body, at the hat that had rolled into the street.

If the hostler was present in the barn, as he must have been, his wish to stay out of it was as strong as the telegrapher's, as Gallant's. Quigley looked frail and lonely as he stood trying to make up his mind. He began to move forward.

Carlin slid into view and shot as he came. Quigley fired a spasmodic shot as each got his bearings, then stiffened in a readier stance. Gallant heard only a single crash of exploding powder, he saw Quigley spin half around and fall. Carlin stood there by the big doors, then came slowly forward and kicked the gun out of Quigley's hand. He hardly paused, coming on toward the main street, looking up just as Gallant jerked back.

In a sick frenzy Gallant wheeled to his desk, yanked open the drawer, and snatched up his gun. He knew beyond question that Carlin would be coming up those stairs in a minute. He hadn't the nerve to face him so, sliding through the outer office, he turned the key in the lock. That only gave him a trapped feeling, a certainty that Carlin would wait outside, wait forever if necessary, to kill him. Gallant hadn't the courage for anything but to unlock the door again and make a run for the back stairs.

He came into the alleyway breathing heavily, looking frantically right and left. It was empty; at that moment Carlin seemed to be in sole possession of the town. Gallant bolted to his left, came right again where the side street ran out into the desert, cut across, and entered the Granger Hotel by its rear door. Padding along the hallway, he was soon back in his private quarters.

He poured himself a stiff drink and downed it. He poured a more temperate one and carried it to his easy chair, where he sank down. As the whisky warmed him, he began to feel ashamed of his panic, at the fact that for the first time in his life he had run from a man. All at once he cursed this Prairie project that was stripping from him the things in which he had once prided himself. He was no match for Carlin with a gun, but his mind was as good as ever.

The shame, being intolerable, began to change to a bright, reckless anger. It was a good thing this had happened, for he knew beyond doubt that Rankin and Quigley were where they could never be made to talk. Carlin had nothing on him. Maybe he hadn't even intended to come up those stairs. The sheriff would come in on the westbound, and if there were any questions Gallant knew that his clerks would help him disavow any connection with the two dead men who had killed old Trevers. Jim Carlin had buttoned the thing up, the sheriff would soon be returning to the county seat.

The state of his nerves, the temper of the town, the rapid vanishing of the summer combined to convince

Gallant that he could no longer wait upon the vagrant whims of Peyt Peyton. It was time he pulled a trick out of his own bag and forced the deadly young cattleman to deliver a ditch agreement. It would take no time at all after that to have things humming. With the start of the irrigation ditch he could draw the money now in escrow. That would permit him to leave overnight if things got out of hand.

Gallant paced the floor while he searched his mind for a way to turn the tables on Peyton. Although he thought his nerves had relaxed, his body jerked when knuckles hit the panel of his door. His first impulse was to ignore it, then, angry with himself, he called out.

"Who is it?"

"Carlin."

The next seconds took a lot out of Gallant. He knew that a show of fear would itself be incriminating. He stepped to the door and turned the key with his left hand, his right on the gun in his coat pocket. Carlin walked in.

His gun was back in its holster. Had Gallant not seen the gun fight that had just taken place he would have thought that the man was completely at ease. Yet the dark eyes—there was something in their depths to tell him that this was still a dangerous man.

Gallant said, "I saw the shooting. What was the trouble?"

"You got back here fast."

"I haven't had my breakfast, and I like to eat here. What can I do for you?"

"You can tell me what kind of deal there is between you and Peyton."

"Deal?" Gallant said, and managed to look surprised. "We've never made one."

"Did he ever tell you that he's got an option to buy

129

the Vassey ranch?"

Gallant couldn't stay on top of that one. He stared hard at Carlin, then recovered and said, "If he's got one, why should he tell me?"

Carlin's smile was cold as blizzard wind. "I didn't think he'd mentioned it," he answered, "let alone warned you to lay off, like he claimed he'd done." He swung and walked out.

Gallant stood with fury consuming him. So he had played the fool for Peyton all along. He knew beyond doubt now that the showdown had come for them all.

CHAPTER 14

TEX RINEHART LOOKED AT THE RECEDING BACK OF THE puncher Peyt had just hired and as the fellow vanished into the bunkhouse with his warbag said, "Another good one. That makes the five you wanted, don't it?"

"That makes it," Peyt said with satisfaction.

They were standing in the headquarters compound after the noon meal. The rider was the last of the lot for which he had written to a saloonman in Sidney, who had always sent up the extra help Crown wanted. The man knew the qualifications, he picked and chose and always sent the best, partly as a favor but also because Boyd had always rewarded him, a practice Peyt meant to continue. He would need a lot of help once the lake country was all Crown range.

"When're we going to spread out?" Tex asked. He sounded eager.

Frowning at him, Peyt said, "When we can. Right now there's enough to keep them all busy. I want to leave plenty of men home to watch our range while

130

we're off on roundup."

He hadn't been over to see Nora for several days, knew she had gone back to Tack, taking Ellen Vassey with her, and decided that it would please her if he took time out during the busy part of the day to drop around. He told Tex to send up the gray he liked to ride on special occasions and went to shave and put on a clean shirt.

Later, as he took the old shore road to Tack, he was thinking that he and Nora, with their pony tracks, had done a lot to help wear it there on the earth, going back and forth when they played together as children, continuing even today. The wedding was very close now, would have taken place before snow flew, and then she would move to Crown to be its mistress. She had been working toward that end all summer, the way women did, sewing things for her hope chest, although he knew it was crammed already, for she had always had womanly gifts, especially with a needle. Soon he would be coming over here only because of the work, for when they were married, if not before, she would turn the spread over to him, keeping out of it as befitted a woman, the way she now did with Bill.

As he came in on the horse, riding through the gap, he had a sense of something being wrong. Then he realized that the brand on the horse grazing in the pasture was the Circle C—Carlin's iron. He frowned, instantly and hotly affronted by the thought that, for some reason, Carlin had been visiting at Tack, then all at once he wondered if something else had happened. He rode on in at a trot.

When Nora failed to rush out to meet him, he knew there was some emergency. He swung down, and as he entered the kitchen she appeared in the inner doorway, so gray-faced and drawn that he knew.

"Nora—what's wrong?" he asked.

She came toward him, and he put his arms about her. "Ellen?"

"Dad."

Even though he had guessed, the swiftness, the confronting reality of it was a shock to Peyt. His arms tightened when he heard her soft sob, then, brokenly, she told him about the cattle stealing Jim had discovered, the trap in which Bill had been caught, the probability that Gallant was back of it, just as he was responsible for Al's death.

"Jim knows who they were and went to wire the sheriff," she concluded. "I don't know why he didn't come back."

"But why didn't you send for me?" he asked.

"Jim was taking care of it."

He stared hard across the top of her head at the blank kitchen wall, the temper returning, and beneath the heat of that was a contrasting cold concern. Carlin had been enough for her at a time when it was reasonable to suppose she would want her future husband, the man she loved. But he knew this was no time to show her his resentment of that and, fearing she would detect his trembling, he stepped back and turned away.

"I'm sorry," he said. "Don't you worry about the work or anything. I'll take care of it. I'll arrange about the—funeral, too."

"Somebody ought to get word to Rye and Martha. They thought so much of Dad."

He wondered irritably if she was trying to send him off. "I'll go up there. Who does Jim think did it?"

"The two men who got away at Red Butte. What puzzles me is why Gallant thought killing Dad would do any good. I'm no more apt to sell Tack than he was."

"Of course not. Gallant knows I wouldn't stand for it, any more than for his buying the Five. It must have been plain rustling. He's too smart to take a dangerous chance like that."

"I'm completely mystified," she said. "Something keeps bothering me."

Again the uneasiness stirred in him, and he wanted to get away before he betrayed something to her. He told her he would be back again in the evening, looked in on Ellen with a consoling word, and left.

He rode on to Fishhook, where he found Rye Jones and his wife taking it easy in the shade of the old cottonwood in their yard. He hadn't been here in years, and Rye climbed to his feet with a look of worry on his features.

"I hope you're just setting the roundup starting date," he said.

"Another man's been killed, Rye."

Rye lifted a hand in protest, then let it fall. "Who this time?"

"Bill."

It seemed to him that Rye's face aged five years in the next breath. The old man returned to his chair and sank into it. Martha sat stricken.

"Not Bill," Rye said, shaking his head.

Peyt told him all he had learned from Nora and, since they would be going down to Tack at once, decided that he would go home by way of Roman Five, not wanting to see the grief in them and Nora and Ellen any more than he had to. He hadn't been this disturbed by Vassey's death because he and Al had been enemies all their lives, but Bill had been a kindly old fellow, not liking the coming marriage but trying to be reasonable about it.

In a voice suddenly harsh Rye said, "There's you and

133

me left, Peyt. Which is next?"

"I don't think this was Gallant, Rye. He knows he can't get the Five, let alone Tack."

"I hope you're right," Rye said doubtfully.

Peyt rode swiftly along the north shore. The two men he had at Five were off somewhere, and he didn't tarry. He got back to Crown to find to his consternation that Rodney Gallant was waiting for him in the ranch office.

Peyt walked in angrily and said, "You fool, haven't you got sense enough not to come here right now?"

Gallant was sitting in the tacky little room's one easy chair smoking a cigar. There was a look in his eye that warned Peyt that a crisis had come.

"I happened to hear about the option you hold on the Vassey ranch," he said.

"And how did you happen to hear that?"

"Carlin told me. He killed two men in Prairie this morning, apparently the rustlers who killed Trevers. He came to see me afterward, obviously to tell me about that option. It seems you've made your neighbors think you secured it just to block me. Yet you never told me. How come?"

"Carlin again!" Peyt breathed, ignoring the question.

"And plenty suspicious of you. So am I, now. Till he told me that, I thought we were working together."

"I never told you to go after the Five."

"You didn't?" Gallant said, and lifted an eyebrow. "I've got a different idea of that. You've used me to further an expansion scheme of your own, nothing else. From here on you're working with me and taking your share of the risks."

"Don't try to give me orders," Peyt said, bristling.

"I'm giving you twenty-four hours to sign a right-of-way agreement," Gallant returned coolly.

"If you think Carlin's suspicions worry me you're

wrong."

Gallant took the cigar from his mouth and studied it. "They could cost you your girl, which means Tack, too, and your chances of buying the Five. They might even get you implicated in the murder of Bill Trevers."

"If they were proved."

"You know Carlin. He'll try to prove them. And 1 can help him do it."

The cool words were like a physical blow to the stomach. Peyt walked over to the chair at the desk and sat down. He made himself laugh. "That would be a real threat if you had any chance to make it good."

"I'll make it good if I don't get that right-of-way by this time tomorrow. I'm confident enough of getting it that I'm wiring the contractor to come on with the men and machinery. I need the money that's in escrow at the bank till the work starts. And, by the way, there's another thing. Rye Jones. Make sure he's not in a position to get an injunction against the ditch and tie it up again. As to the two women, I take it you can handle them."

"What makes you so sure of yourself?" Peyt demanded.

Gallant pulled a paper from the inside of his coat, unfolded it, and tossed it over. "That's a copy, and the original's in safekeeping, so it won't do you any good to tear it up. Read it."

Peyt read the brief document with widening eyes, then dropped it on the desk and hammered it hard with his fist. "A forgery!" he exploded. "You've taken your name off the agreement you got from Morgan to turn the Red Butte claim over to you if it proved necessary. You put my name on. It won't get you anything, Gallant." Contemptously he tossed it back.

"You think I can't make it look authentic? Rankin got

this off Morgan's body and sold it to me, figuring I might need it. He was right." Gallant lifted an eyebrow. "That sounds valid enough, doesn't it?"

Peyt swung around the desk. He grasped the front of Gallant's shirt and tried to haul him out of the chair. Gallant struck the hand down, said, "Stand back, Peyton," and Peyt wheeled to the window and stared out, his chest heaving. Then he turned around.

"All right, use it, but it won't hold up."

Gallant laughed. "Not in court, but that's not where I mean to use it. Think it over." He rose leisurely and walked out to where his buggy waited. He wasn't pretending, he was very sure of success.

Peyt got a bottle out of his desk and took a pull. He was afraid that Gallant had him, that while the charges might not be believed by Nora she would not entirely disbelieve them, either. He dared not risk it, he had to comply with Gallant's demands or find a way to offset the damage he could do. He took another drink before he quit shaking.

Going to the window, he saw riders moving along the lake road, heading west, and recognized Carlin with the sheriff, knew they were coming out from Prairie. They didn't deepen his fear by turning in, steadily moving on toward Tack.

Suddenly all the hatred he had ever felt was focused on Carlin. Maybe he had planted suspicions in Nora's mind already, which was why she had not turned to him in her trouble. The man must have poisoned her thoughts, ingratiated himself with her, maybe wanting the ranch as much as he wanted her.

His wrath turned then to Gallant. He wouldn't give in to him or anybody else, he had been in the saddle too long to feel its weight on his own back. Then all at once the rebellion died. He had pressed too hard for that option, even though Nora had herself suggested it, he should have held off longer. He shouldn't have let her see his reluctance to tear it up when she asked. He shouldn't have been fool enough to let Carlin catch him in Gallant's office. Then the horrifying thought struck him that Carlin and the sheriff would have seen Gallant on the Prairie road, so close as yet to Crown they would know where he had been. Peyt smashed the desk again with his fist.

He walked to the door and shouted for Tex Rinehart, who was with a crew of men shoeing horses for roundup. When the foreman came in, he said, "You saw Gallant here."

"Sure."

"All right. You were worried about his being here, knowing how hostile I've been toward him ever since Vassey was killed. So you slipped up outside the office and listened. You heard him threaten to frame me with a forged paper if I didn't sell him his right-of-way in twenty-four hours."

"So?"

"Tell anybody who happens to ask, even me if I ask you in front of somebody else. And it's the truth, Tex. That's just what he threatened to do. The only thing is, I didn't have a witness. You're it."

"I'm it," Tex agreed.

The panic was gone, Peyt felt like himself again. The natural, effective thing was to beat Gallant to the punch, tell Nora, Carlin, and anybody else who happened to be on Tack how he had been threatened. That would turn the tables; he could go on from there and suggest that he buy the Five at once as his answer to Rodney Gallant.

"I want another horse," he said to Tex.

137

When he reached Nora's place, Carlin, the sheriff, and Rye had gone on to the chop hills, where Bill had been shot. Peyt could scarcely believe his luck. Seated on the porch with Nora, he told her of Gallant's crude attempt at blackmail, how he had told him where to head in.

"The idea of him thinking you and Ellen would believe that," he said, and laughed.

"Why don't you give her back the option, Peyt?" Nora asked. "That would prove your good intentions better than anything you could say."

The elation that had burned perhaps too high was completely gone. He didn't dare refuse again, he couldn't even discuss that, and there was only one other resort. He took it. Staring at her hotly, he said, "Gallant could have fooled you, I see. Who poisoned your mind—Carlin?"

"Why, nobody did," she cried.

"He wants you," he resumed fiercely before she could go on. "I've known it from the day he came here. He'd do anything to get you, turn you against me. And you're falling for it. There's no other explanation."

"Peyt, you listen to me—"

He laughed harshly. "I'm glad I know. Gallant's paper still won't do him any good, because you already believe what he would try to make you. I'll be happy to tell him that when he comes back for his answer."

All at once she quit trying to argue, only sat looking at him numbly, pulling, it seemed to him, a thousand miles away. But he dared not let her get him in another corner. He walked to his horse, went astride, and rode off.

He rode arrogantly until he was through the gap and on the lake shore, where he reined in. He was still breathing heavily, and a feeling of entrapment had ridden with him all the way from the house. Where was the sleek adroitness with which he had got so far with his plans? He knew in that moment that he might have to give them up, his lifelong ambitions with them, or lose her. And to Carlin, which made it all the more an intolerable thing.

As he sat there he remembered how he had been caught this way before when Bill proposed marriage to Ellen. He had got out of that one, although he no longer had Gallant to bait and nudge into taking the necessary steps. Now Carlin stood in the way, not Bill, and there was a way to remove him, too.

CHAPTER 15

WHEN JIM, BOB LANDORF, AND RYE JONES REACHED Boiler Spring they made a careful inspection of the premises and, before long, found where men had laid in wait for Bill Trevers.

"So my hunch was right," Jim said darkly. "This proves it was murder from start to finish, that rustling only set it up."

Landorf shifted the weight of his stocky body in the saddle. "I wish it did prove it."

"Why don't it?" Rye asked hotly. "They weren't caught in the act by Bill, in which case there'd be more sense to killing him. They set a deliberate deadfall, and the sign here shows it. Why'd they do that?"

"To kill him," Landorf agreed. "I see it the way you do, but all we've got is a theory and two dead men in Prairie. Jim, you can't even prove they were resisting a citizen's arrest."

"Gallant saw me from his office window," Jim

retorted. "If he lies about it, that proves they had his backing."

"But you're the one in trouble if he claims they were defending themselves against you."

"There was the livery man."

"He's already said the first he knew there was trouble was when he heard the shooting. The depot man watched the windup but didn't see it start. You saw, the same as I did, that the Prairie people lean to the dead men's side. They scoff at the rustling charge, claim you were out to get the men Vassey didn't kill."

"Somebody around there was buying Tack meat," Rye exploded. "And from Rankin and Quigley."

"Or, which is more likely, from a go-between," Landorf said tiredly. "Believe me, I'd like to lay this thing out for what it is, but I don't think I'll have much luck."

They rode on into the sand hills to look over the situation there. In spite of the Tack cattle, the wagon tracks, the evidence of butchering, Jim began to feel the frustration the law officer was experiencing. There was nobody but himself to claim the guilty persons were Rankin and Quigley, which could be dismissed as a flimsy attempt to justify his killing them.

"I'm going to follow those wagon tracks and see where they lead," Landorf decided. "But I don't think you boys ought to show up in Prairie till you have to. It might start more trouble. But be there for the inquest in the morning, Jim. I'm holding Bill's body for it, too. The undertaker's going to bring him in. Might as well tell you I've got a feeling they'll make you face a grand jury as well, and they'll be the grand jury."

"I know," Jim answered.

When he had returned to Boiler with Jim, Rye said, "You go straight home from here. If a man ever had a

140

right to look beat out you have, and you sure do. Martha and me'll stay at Tack, at least she can. You get some sleep."

"I guess I'd better," Jim agreed. "But I don't feel like I could sleep or eat again. What's gone wrong with this country, Rye? It's running crazy."

"Nesters is what's wrong with it," Rye spat. "Let 'em show up and trouble starts, every trip. You get along."

Nodding, Jim rode southwest toward the sink of the Dry, reflecting that settlers were not all that had gone wrong with the lake country. His suspicion that Peyt was at best playing a two-faced game had been confirmed that morning by Gallant himself. The nature of that game kept tugging at his mind, engendering in the deeper nerves of his body a feeling he did not like to entertain. It would have gained Gallant nothing to order Bill killed unless he felt sure of later cooperation from Peyt, and Gallant had been on Crown just today. When Jim considered that and the quick way Peyt had secured an option on the Five, although encouraged in it by Nora, he had a feeling that Gallant himself might have been made a tool in two murders as cold-blooded as could be imagined.

The thought of mentioning this to Nora, of warning her, was untenable. Yet unless the plan was knocked in the head immediately and the guilty ones exposed, Rye stood in imminent peril, perhaps the ranchers on the Cutbank and Red Butte as well. All the way to the sink he tried to find a plan to counteract that danger, without success, while also yearning to bring to account the men really responsible for Bill's and Al's deaths.

When he came to the low eastern bluff of his sink he stopped his horse before starting down, his tired gaze playing over its expanse, knowing it was jeopardized

141

equally as much as the other outfits so far untouched. As he sat in this discouragement he had a rising dread of what might come of the fight in Prairie. In his anger he had discounted it, but now he was moved by a sense that he had not begun to see the extent of the trouble.

When Rye returned to Tack, gently insisting that she get some rest, Nora went to her own room and lay down on the bed. Grief and fatigue had numbed her, and though she tried to relax it was impossible. Yet in this privacy, where it was not necessary to fight them back, she felt tears rise in her eyes. The world had ended, there was nothing but emptiness in her with Bill gone, and instead of her gaining comfort from Peyt he had only grown angry and left her completely miserable.

Yet he had asked a question she now let herself consider. Why had she felt no need to send for him immediately when she could have done so by Jim? It occurred to her that everything she herself needed from a man, at least of which she was conscious, she had found in her father; her sense of security had come from Bill and not from Peyt, and when he died she had been left without anybody to lean on.

Then, as she pondered, the insistent thought broke through that this was not entirely true, for Jim had been there and, although she had not realized it, she had at once transferred this natural dependence to him. It was still attached to Jim. Somehow the thought of his being near had helped. It still helped whenever she considered the hard days that lay ahead for her.

It dawned on her then that everyone save herself and Peyt had to some degree sensed the unnaturalness of their feeling, that she got from it only what she could get in time from her own children, that Bill had supplied the rest of her needs, that it had taken the two of them to do what a man like Jim could do naturally and at once. Perhaps not just a man like Jim, but Jim only—she was too exhausted to feel very much for anybody just then.

She wanted Bill's funeral held immediately after the law was done with him, and afterward there would be many new problems. Peyt would naturally run Tack, adding it to Crown as he would now add the Five. Her home would become a Crown line camp for men to batch in while they took care of that part of the range. Roman Five would likewise be demoted, while Crown grew bigger. The guilty, unworthy question rose in her mind as to how much that bigness meant to Peyt. She was still convinced that she had herself inspired him to it, but there was no doubting that it had taken hold.

All at once she could not bear to think about anything, and thus her mind grew still. Presently she slept.

It seemed to her it was no time at all until she opened her eyes to notice that the light in the room had softened. Then she realized someone was talking on the porch beyond the wall and she heard Rye say, "She's asleep, Peyt, and she needs the rest."

Rising quickly from the bed, Nora rushed to the open window to see Peyt still in the saddle, about to turn his horse. She called to him, then fled through the house and out. Rye returned grumpily indoors, displeased that they had disturbed her.

Peyt wore the contrite look she knew so well. He said, "I could have come back later. I just wanted to say I'm sorry I flew off the handle at the worst possible time. I'd have brought the option back to Ellen but it's in the bank. I'll get it tomorrow."

Instantly uncertain of her own attitude about that,

Nora said, "She's got to sell. I only thought, from what you said about Gallant's threat to frame you, that you should make the offer."

"I'm making it now. Can I go in and see her?"

She nodded, and he swung out of the saddle, then suddenly she grew doubtful of the wisdom of such a gesture. She said, "Maybe you'd better wait, Peyt. She's got to sell to you or Gallant now. If she got the idea you don't want to buy the place she'd be in an awful position. I guess it bothered me that you were so against it."

"I'm not against it. You made me feel you didn't trust me. But if you think I'd better not say anything to her I won't."

She would have been put at rest about it had she not had a feeling he was relieved by her decision, that he had made his offer hoping she would remember how it might look to Ellen. Shame rose in her again, then immediately she wondered whether it was a guilty thought or simple clarity come to her at long last about him. She looked up into his face and saw its willfulness, its immaturity. She remembered the many times she had angered him only to have him come back because he could not get along without her.

The only reason he's drawn to me or ever was, she thought in wonder, is that I've always had milk for him.

He stepped forward then and took her in his arms, and although she thought it was her weariness she felt no lift at all when he kissed her mouth. Then the ultimate honesty came to her and she knew that she never would again, that something had changed in her, that she was no longer one of two youngsters with a vital need for each other.

As he rode out she watched after him, realizing anew the weight of the responsibility she had always felt for him. A change in her own feeling did not alter that; too

144

many memories went into the obligation for it to be abolished by a change in herself. She would marry him because it was not in her nature to fail him, and once the terrible things that were happening were forgotten they would be happy in each other as they once had been.

The resolution settled the disturbance that had been in her ever since she grew aware that the Five had meant more to him all along than she had ever supposed.

As he moved along the south shore, riding leisurely, Peyt knew he had not succeeded in regaining the hold he had always had on Nora. With his mind firmly made up on what his next step would be, it had been necessary to try to do so. He had gambled that she would not press her desire for him to relinquish his hold on the Five; had that failed, he would have stalled about getting the option out of the bank. She hadn't required it, yet she hadn't returned to him, either.

He still held Carlin strictly to blame for her rebellion against him, knew with cold realism that in the run of time Carlin would take her away from him. Therefore, when he reached Crown to find the crew washing up for supper, he called the foreman into the office.

He poured drinks for two and looked at Tex through a thoughtful moment.

"What four men in the outfit," he asked presently, "do you trust the most?"

"Depends on what for."

"To do a job and keep their mouths shut afterward."

"I can't count that many," Tex decided. "They'll all do what they're told, but there's only two or three I'd want to give any kind of hold on me."

"That'll have to do," Peyt said. "You can make another and I'll complete the hand, though I didn't want to."

"What're we going to do?"

"Give the Dry sink back to nature."

Tex came forward in his chair, his eyes gleaming. He tossed off the drink and put the glass on the desk. "So you're taking on the champ. When?"

"Tonight. First I want a nester plug picked up, and one of those pads they use when they ride."

"It's going to look like nester work?"

"As much as we can make it. Carlin killed two men in Prairie. After the Red Butte don't you think they'd look for blood themselves?"

"Man would think so," Tex agreed. "We going to burn him out?"

"We're going to wipe him out. I know that'll cost me money—you and the others. You'll get it. Be damned sure the men you pick are to be trusted, and don't let anybody else know. Have them slip off one at a time and meet at Indian Well."

"Who's going to get the nester horse?"

"You and me. That homestead at Rooster Rock ought to be a good place to try for it. Now let's go get supper."

He ate with good appetite and afterward, astride a fresh horse, rode out on the old Moccasin trail. But once he had topped the rise he turned slantwise into a stand of trees where he swung down to wait for Tex. Seating himself, he rolled a cigarette and lighted it, drawing in the first puffs with pleasure. Of all the things he had done and caused to happen, nothing could afford him a keener satisfaction than this night, which had been in the back of his mind from the day Boyd Peyton died.

He knew with deep gratification that Boyd might have planned but would never have found the courage to carry out such an expansion of Crown holdings as was now all but accomplished. He had made Gallant's

146

threat meaningless and looked forward to telling him so. Now he felt no obligation to the man at all, would let him go bankrupt. Afterward more reliable men—regular Prairie business people—would enlist willingly in a sound irrigation project that would draw the settlers away from the new Crown, furnish a permanent market for the water he would control himself, thus controlling everything.

In a way he had done what they accused Boyd of doing in Custer County so long ago, not only saving but improving himself in an apparently ruinous situation. Yet he had accomplished it with a difference that removed the stigma from Crown, from the Peyton name. Even though he was the only one who knew all about it, that was enough, for removing that shame from his own memory was the essential part of it.

A little later Tex came in through the deepening night, and Peyt swung back into the saddle. Rooster Rock lay on toward the railroad on what had been part of the old nester-devoured Crow Track, and they reached it in about an hour. Peyt had picked it because the settler was a bachelor, and all of that breed went to bed with the fall of night. There was a team in the barn, no dog, and looking about, they found a riding pad and put it on one of the horses. Leading the stolen horse, they rode out again, heading for Indian Well.

Three men waited there, smoking in the darkness. Swinging down, Peyt said, "We'll rest awhile. Carlin might have taken it in his head to go back to Tack. We'll give him plenty of time to get home again."

"What are you going to do with that crowbait?" a man asked nodding toward the nester horse.

"Leave it at Circle C with a bullet in its head."

Peyt began to key up as they waited at the well. Tex

147

had picked Bill Draper, Tod Webster, and Harry New, special cronies of his, and they were tough fighting men, apparently more used to this kind of work than Peyt was himself. They talked among themselves, mostly of women and card hands and rough exploits. Peyt respected them for their hard outlooks yet despised them for their lack of ambition beyond the gratification of vagrant appetites. Once the cloud had passed from Crown and all was well and safe, he would get rid of them, even Tex, because they would be too dangerous to him. He smiled in the darkness to himself, wondering what they would do about it if they could see into his mind.

CHAPTER 16

ONCE HE MANAGED TO FALL ASLEEP JIM WAS LIKE A drugged man. When he awakened, the soddy's interior was dark, the outer light from a star-dusted sky falling through the three windows of his one-room sodhouse so that he could see its simple furnishings, the stove across from the bunk, the table at its end, and all the clutter of several years of bachelor living. His head ached, a dull throb at the base of his neck, and it seemed to him that in the moment of awakening the tensions he had subdued but not thrown off roiled up to sweep the last relaxed peace from his mind. He hadn't eaten when he came in, instead stretching out on the bunk with only his dusty boots removed, and he decided that, whatever the hour, he needed to fix himself at least the excuse of a meal.

He sat up on the bunk, his feet on the floor, and rubbed the back of his neck. Yawning then, he looked at

148

the stove and vaguely wondered why he smelled smoke when there had been no fire in it all day. His mind jumped forward to another possibility and he sprang erect.

From the front window he could see out through the cottonwoods to the gnawed, gashed bed of Dry Creek. All was serene out there, not brightly lighted, vaguely reposed in the night's quiet. Then he swung to look out the window at the end of the room, giving to the south, and pure horror slashed through him.

Down at the edge of the sink a yellow mass shimmered against a black background, it brightened and faded, and even as he watched it seemed to spread. He had noted coming in that the wind was from that direction, it had carried smoke to him, the warning of what he had always feared here in the middle of his hayland—a grass fire.

Wheeling numbly to the bunk, he sat down to pull on his boots, trying to think what he might do. Whatever had started the thing, it was sheer disaster for it to break out there, upwind from the wheeling sea of his winter hay. He fought panic and forced himself to cold reason. The only thing that might save the sink, his buildings, everything, was a backfire ignited quickly up there, so that the back draft could burn off a fire belt.

He stamped his feet on into his boots as he whipped to the door and flung it open. In that instant a shot rang out, a bullet tearing into the door, jarring it, instinct throwing him back inside. He shut the door hastily as the gun fired again, the lead tore through the panel and hit the sod blocks of the back wall. He swayed as if it had hit him, but only from the utter, disbelieving shock of the situation. He hadn't thought until then that the fire had been set deliberately. It was now shakingly clear

149

that he was not to be permitted to fight it.

Drawing in a sharp breath, he slid to the corner and caught up his rifle, trembling, not yet in command of himself. A glance through the south window showed him a strengthening light. Some dozen old cottonwoods stood along the creek on the front side of the house; the gunman was in among them somewhere covering the sodhouse's one door. Padding to the south window, Jim looked out at the benighted shape of his barn, the corral at its end, past which he could see the growing fire, and remembered that the whole sweep between these structures and the house was exposed to gunfire from the creek trees.

The back window was his only chance, although that side of his headquarters was all open save for a couple more trees. Slipping across to that sash, he reached up and pulled out the pegs that held it in its casing, lifted the sash out, and placed it on the floor. Nothing happened, but a more settled wariness prompted him to find his hat and hold it in the empty window space. A gun crashed out and the hat was torn from his grasp. He cursed bitterly, knowing there were several men, that they had him hemmed in. Settlers from Prairie, seeking revenge? He didn't know, nor did it matter at that moment for he had to get out of there somehow.

He moved quietly to the north window, which showed him the main part of the sink, running on toward the narrows and then Tack's range. This also was open land except for four or five trees standing at lonely distances, one not a hundred feet from the corner of the house. He saw a man watching carefully from there and, jerking the rifle to his shoulder, he threw a savage shot through the window glass. The only positive result was that the man cut back and did not venture to look again.

The door was covered, and Jim knew by then that if he tried to lift himself through one of the three windows he would die before he had got started. They wouldn't rush him, they needed only to hold him there until the spreading fire came down the sink and got into the buildings. Then he would be driven out, and they would have him.

He cursed the lack of a front window, and had to give himself a chance to get at the men there, which offered the faintest of hope that he might be able to make a run into the creek trees. Moving up to the hinged side of the door, he reached out, drew back the bar, and let the door swing open. Half a dozen angry shots rang out in the foreground; Jim decided there were at least two men on that side although from where he stood he could see nothing.

He knew also that they could not see very far into the soddy. He moved across to the far wall and began to edge along it, seeking as much interior darkness as he could get. He was exposed to fire, and if they raked the area where he was they were bound to get him. But, expecting an attempt to dash out now that the door stood open, they held fire. They were playing a wary game with every advantage on their side and wasting no opportunities for the sake of sportsmanship. Sweeping up a straight-back chair, he hurled it toward the opening, instantly following.

The ruse gave him the small advantage he hoped for; somebody threw a shot at the sailing chair in a startled reflex, he spotted the powder flash and drove a rifle bullet toward it. A man yelled. But a second gun poured fire into the doorway itself, driving Jim back.

The whole south window had by then turned red, the smoke drifted in to mix with that of gunpowder, making him cough. A terrible despair laid on his mind for a second. His pasture was fenced, there were half a dozen horses in there, and even now the flames must be reaching the pasture's south edge. Desperation wiped out the despairing as he thought of the animals stampeding and tearing themselves to pieces on the barbed wire. That seemed worse to him than the loss of his winter hay, his buildings.

He had to fight himself to keep from making a run through the door, shooting as he went. He had got in one good shot, hoped it had done some damage, and had located the tree shielding a second gunman. He had to keep cool enough to try for him before he threw everything into the pot. They wouldn't fall for anything tossed out again, but no man had complete control of his nerves at a time like this.

In the quiet he could hear the beat of hoofs on the earth, knew his horses were racing about the pasture seeking an opening they could not find.

He yelled, "At least turn out those horses!"

The answer was a jumpy shot; he saw the flash and fired into it. He heard a man's sharp outcry. He drilled in a second shot before the other man out there drove him back, disclosing that to that point there had still been two in the fight.

He stood there choking in the smoky, fumes-hung air, knowing by then that everything in the sink was doomed, that he now fought for his life. The attackers would themselves be driven out once the flames reached close, would probably break for the bluff and mount to the bench, which he could not gain in time himself without a horse, making their devastation complete. Yet rebellion rode him for he was not a man to see the work of five hard years, the expectancy of a lifetime, wiped out in such a manner.

He stood edged to the door where it hinged, hoping somebody on that side would expose himself. The droning roar of the fire was a steady racket, and in this sound suddenly he heard the crash of weight against the wire fence and immediately the agonizing outbursts of a horse's scream. He nearly went out the door then heedlessly. But he managed to hold onto himself, his stinging eyes searching hungrily.

All at once he swung back into the dark interior. Pulling off his shirt, he tore it into sections, then bundled the whole together as rags. Assured that the men outside would not rush him when they could wait until he had to emerge, he worked thoroughly. Groping about until he found a stick of wood, he wrapped and roughly knotted the rags about one end. Unscrewing the wick of the coal oil lamp, he poured the lamp's contents over the rags. Breathing heavily, occasionally having to cough, he found his gun belt and buckled it on. From the shelf over the stove he took extra cartridges for the rifle and dropped them into his pocket. Then he swung the door shut.

Wiping a match across the stove top, he lighted the firebrand, holding it a moment while it caught well, hearing a shot knock out a suddenly lighted window. Moving to the handle side of the door, he turned the brand over in his hand to make sure it was burning in earnest. Using his left hand to jerk the door open, he threw the brand overhand, out into the dry grass on the upwind side of the trees. A bullet crashed into the doorjamb as he yanked himself back.

Out of their line of fire, he saw that the burning torch had landed neatly in the grass between the two leftmost trees, where they could not interfere with it without exposing themselves in its scattered light. He saw the

153

grass catch fire, and his lips pulled tight to his teeth. Somebody, keeping himself protected by a tree, flung a couple of useless shots into the new fire. The little grass patch there through the trees would burn out quickly, but they would have to pull back. He would have to guess when that had happened and make his try. If, one way or another, he could reach the bed of the creek he would have a much better chance to take care of himself.

All at once the strengthening fire seemed to burst forward toward the trees. That, if anything, would cause them to scramble out of there, and Jim took his chance. Plunging out the door, he made first for the corner of the house, only to be shot at from the barn. Speeding in zigzag runs, he reached a tree south of the fire he had set, and there was no one else there. He threw a shot at the barn from that point, sped for a second tree, then was over the bank of the creek.

He lay panting, the smoke out here worse than in the house. He had made a gain, but since his first objective was to reach the barn the progress was offset by the discovery that a man had posted himself there. Figuring this might be the last chance he would have, he replaced the empties in the rifle, then moved on a distance down the Dry bed until he was abreast a tree he knew to stand against the back corner of his corral.

The fire in the trees seemed to have covered his movements from all but the man in the barn, who now jeopardized his next step. He crawled up the bank and in under the cottonwood tree, and there saw his horses bunched and milling about the gate. He understood for the first time why the big fire, capable of a speed as fast as a running horse, had not yet engulfed headquarters. The cropped grass of the pasture had checked it at the south fence, but only temporarily for it was eating to the

154

side in both directions. Once it had lapped around the corners of the pasture it would quickly regain its vigor and roar up on the sink.

His first intention had been to try to release the trapped, terrified horses, trying to catch one by the mane and ride it out. Suddenly an unexpected opportunity confronted him. If he could backfire down the sides of the pasture he might hold the fire in its present position, for the cliffs would contain it on one side and the wide creek bed on the other. They were bound to kill him before he could manage it, but if through some miracle he made it he could save his headquarters and a good part of his hay.

He dropped back into the bed of the creek and headed downstream. Nobody back at the house was firing pot shots at anything; he knew he had them baffled, an immunity that could be destroyed instantly if he attracted attention by setting a new fire. He didn't hesitate in doing that, moving out of the creek at a point about halfway along the pasture's side fence. It was the work of a minute to set two spot fires in the dry wild grass. There was little chance of their going out, but he waited to be sure they caught. At first they spread outward, but by then the larger fire had created a centrific thermal draft that affected the spot fires. In a moment they were crackling and running south.

Slipping between the strands of barbed wire, Jim struck across the open horse pasture on the run. If they guessed his purpose and swung back onto their horses to come after him, he would never make it. The smoke was choking but helped conceal, perhaps mask him completely. Sweat began to stream from him from the heat and running, brands settled on his naked shoulders and stung like hornets. The smoke grew denser as he

155

progressed, and all at once he nearly ran into the opposite fence.

A defiant elation rose in him as he got through the fence and repeated his work. Because of the smoke he couldn't tell what the other fire was doing. The thought came to him now that if he moved on to the bluffs and worked his way back he might come upon their horses. The chance of setting them afoot, if not capturing them, was too compelling to dismiss. His lungs aching from the smoke, he started out, moving more slowly so as to conserve air.

The cliff's low, ragged rises were about two hundred yards from the pasture fence. He came to them in the smoky night and found no relieving fresh air. Panting and gagging, he began to move north, figuring they would have left their mounts at the bottom of the notch he always used when climbing to the table. He doubted they would be nester plugs; he wanted to see the brands.

All at once he froze in horror as a rosy daub stained the night ahead. He hauled up, his mouth open and gasping, staring with stinging, streaming eyes. Scrambling a little higher on the talus, he got a better view and knew in cold shock that they had offset his backfires by setting new ones to the north. The flames were now rushing down directly upon the trees and his buildings.

Jim Carlin went wild, unable to accept that, springing down from the rock on which he stood and driving in toward the buildings. He saw a man running through the smoke, a brief glimpse that was gone before he could shoot. He knew they were running toward their horses, having little time to get out of there, but at the moment he could think only of his own trapped animals.

By the time he gained the pasture fence he saw he

was too late to reach the gate; the fire on that side already burned along the fence, was all but upon the side of the barn. Using the barrel of his rifle, he got a purchase on the wire where he was, began to turn the gun, twisting until the tightening wire snapped. He broke the other strands and laid them back. Running into the pasture, he raced toward the horses, which now pressed together against the barn's back wall, fire burning on three sides of them. He hazed them toward the opening, and when they saw it they went charging through. He had given no thought at all to his own escape.

Instead he plunged on into the yard. Another year would bring another hay crop, but his buildings and belongings were the fruit of many years. There were grain sacks in the barn, and he found a couple, dashing on with them to his well. Wetting the burlap in the trough, he rounded the end of the barn, ignoring the searing heat, and began to flail the burning grass at its advancing edge. He could feel his hair singe, and his naked upper body, though sweat-soaked, seemed to broil in the intense heat.

All at once the whole side of the barn burst into flame, stunning him with its sudden completeness. As if the superheated boards gave off some kind of combustible vapor, the fire spewed and lapped upward to the roof. Hardly aware that he was himself cooking, he watched the hungry flames curl over onto the roof. His head reeling, blinded by sweat and heat, he stumbled out into the more open yard.

The soddy, built when he lacked the money for lumber, had a combustible roof, although its walls could withstand the intense heat. There was no grass about it, and he had a better chance than with the barn. Running

157

to the shed in back, he found his ladder and put it up against the outside wall. Wetting the sacks again, he mounted the roof to put out any fire that might ignite in the peatlike mixture of straw and earth up there.

From that viewpoint he found himself surrounded by a sea of fire, escape cut off, and knew that nothing, not even his life, could now be saved from it.

CHAPTER 17

RYE JONES HAD STAYED LATE AT TACK, WHERE Martha was remaining overnight, but because he had neglected his own work he saddled his horse around ten o'clock to return to Fishhook alone. He had just broke up out of the creek bed, at the ford, when he saw, far south, the hint of fire against the night sky. He had a special horror of a grass fire, having lost two sons in a single scourging hour, and for an instant he stared in stupefaction, feeling sick at his stomach, remembering the day tragedy had come to him and Martha Then his mind started working and he drew a sharp breath.

"That's in the sink!" he said aloud. "It's Jim's hay!"

Anywhere that grass stood high and dry a man could expect such a thing at any time, but now as he swung the horse south and hit it with his spurs Rye remembered all the other things that had happened around the lake since Gallant set out to gain access to its water. He had a strong hunch that Jim was in serious trouble not of nature's creating.

Back in the narrows he could not see the glow, yet he rode at a speed he had not equaled in many years. The hoofs of the racing horse kicked sparks out of the gravel, the creek brush whipped past, and each moment

158

dragged into an hour of normal living as his feeling mounted that Jim was in danger. He kept using the spurs, he kept grunting and encouraging "Hah-hah" that seemed to bring the best from the horse, and presently he could smell smoke. As at long last he came out of the narrows he saw the appalling spread of leaping fire across the entire sink, and by then the smoke was thick enough to torment him.

That sight told him there was no saving the hay, that Jim's buildings might already be destroyed. He drew up for a moment to consider his own course, since he could not continue very far along the bottom. Then he cut slantwise toward the bluffs, saw that it would be difficult if not impossible to ride along their base, but did so until he found a cleft where he could top out to the bench. Thereafter he began to ride harder.

As he bore down upon Jim's regular route of reaching and leaving the bench he pulled up his horse in a sliding halt, for horses were breaking out of the bottom, emerging from the smoke, and he understood at once that they were enemies. Like the others, he had worn a gun ever since the deadly nature of the water conflict became apparent, but here in the open one man with poor eyesight was no match against the five riders he saw rim out and cut northeast.

As he watched them he revised his count; there were five horses but one, led, had an empty saddle. Yet it was not empty, he decided as his aging eyes focused more sharply, for something lay across it, the body of a hurt or dead man. That told him that Jim had put up a fight, was still down there in that sea of fire and smoke, himself wounded or dead. He was sure of one other thing, the fleeing horsemen all rode like experts, which put down his first natural suspicion of the nesters.

They had not noticed him, and because he wanted to help Jim if possible he remained motionless, only a fixed speck in the prairie night, until distance had swallowed them. Then, gigging his horse, he cut for the notch and went down into the smoke and heat. The fire burned almost upon the belowground, although he saw it only as a rolling, red-stained mass of black. As he stared at it through streaming eyes he had his moment of sick fear, in which memory of the red day that had blackened his life rose before him. For that instant the thought stood cogently in his mind that Jim probably was past helping, that it was folly to add another life to the cost of this thing. Yet he knew at the same time that he would accept no guesswork in a matter so vital, and he put his horse on down the short grade.

The horse made a low protesting whistle and tried to turn back until Rye spurred it savagely. Yet the animal's instinct was right for all at once the whole stretch below burst into flame spontaneously. Rye turned back and scrambled out of there, cursing the fire, the night riders, his helplessness. Then a thought entered his mind: if he made his way south a short distance he might be able to cut across the burned-over area into the horse pasture, where the cropped grass would have resisted the fire, and that might let him reach the buildings—or the place where they had been.

It was hard going along the rough talus, it took time. Then the smoke thinned notably and he could see below him a strip of glowing char that told him the fire had not seriously invaded the pasture. Greatly enheartened, he put the horse on down, quirting it with the ends of his reins to the edge of the char, where it balked completely. Rye swung out of the saddle and left the animal. The ground heated his boots painfully as he raced across it, but without the horse he had the advantage of being able to go through the fence into the pasture. Smoke hung across the whole area but was then thin enough he could see the raging red hulk of Jim's burning barn. Rye plunged on.

The heat of the barn forced him to the right, and he found a place where somebody had broken open the fence, probably to let the horses out of the pasture. He went through and saw the burning roof of Jim's soddy. He began to shout, "Jim—Jim!" but there was no answer. He raced to the open door of the soddy, and just as he came to it the roof collapsed while he kept yelling for Jim, getting nothing back but the chuckling roar of the flames. The sick thought streaked through his mind that Jim probably had been hurt or killed in the house, that he was under that burning roof.

Rye swung to try to get out of the area himself when he saw a man's arm hanging over the side of the water trough.

Racing toward the trough, he saw the unconscious form of the man he sought, all but the face submerged in the water. Rye let out a bleat of relief, knowing Jim had crawled in there when heat from the burning grass and buildings was its most intense, that a wound, or maybe combustion gas, had knocked him out. Rye lifted him and, not pausing, ran back toward the horse pasture, knowing that an area like this entrapped deadly vapors that could drop a man before he knew of their presence.

Rye's gaunt frame had once carried tremendous power, and now the power came back from somewhere to help him. Somehow he carried a man heavier than himself across the yard, the pasture, and got him through the fence. He began to stagger and reel as he recrossed the burned area for it was still intensely hot, its lingering smoke as deadly as elsewhere. He was completely soaked from Jim's dripping and his own profuse sweat when he reached the horse. He threw Jim across the saddle, secured him with a pigging string, then began to lead the horse along the rough talus, stumbling and falling and getting up to go on again.

It seemed forever before he reached the grade and could climb up out of the smoke and heat. When he and the burdened horse had topped out Rye fell flat and lay there with his old lungs heaving, his heart racing so he wondered why, at its age, it did not burst and kill him. He kept retching, but presently this stopped, his pulse slowed, and his breathing steadied. He got to his feet, untied Jim, and lifted him down from the saddle. With the unconscious man stretched on the grass, Rye began to chafe his wrists, enormously relieved that there was no evident wound.

The fresh air quickly restored Jim, as it had Rye. Jim made a low groaning sound, then all at once lifted onto his elbows, looking about wildly.

"It's all right, Jim," Rye said.

"Rye!" Jim gasped disbelievingly. He lay back, his eyes closed again, and Rye thought for a moment that he had slipped back into his stupor. But after resting thus a little longer Jim sat up.

"It's gone, Rye," he said. "Everything's gone."

"I know. And if you hadn't crawled into that trough you'd be gone with it. Who was it?"

"I never saw a man close enough to say. Nesters, maybe. Because of Rankin and Quigley."

"They sure didn't ride like sodbusters."

"You saw them?"

"From a distance." Rye unconsciously pulled tobacco from his pocket, then looked at it with distaste, feeling he would never care to smoke again.

All at once Jim said sharply, "You must have gone down into it and got me, Rye. For a minute I thought I'd got up here by myself somehow. But you said trough. I crawled into that, then everything went blooey."

"I got in there easy," Rye said.

"I bet."

Jim explained then how he had been sleeping when they moved in around his house, how he had discovered the fire and nearly walked into a bullet, afterward breaking out and setting backfires, only to have them put the torch anew to the unburned area, dooming everything.

"I think you got one," Rye said. "Somebody rode home on his belly."

"Once when I shot I heard a yell."

"By God," Rye decided, "Gallant's brought in a fresh gun crew. That's the only thing that makes sense. I thought me or Peyt would be next on his list. Why you, I wonder."

"Practice, maybe," Jim said bitterly. He rose to his feet and walked over to the rim.

Rye followed. By then the breeze was carrying off the smoke until they could see the southern part of the sink, now a black, flat, red-dotted carpet in the starlight. Directly out from them the barn and house still burned. On north the flames at last had reached the bluffs, where they would pinch out at the narrows. In another hour it would all be over, a fine little ranch destroyed.

"Well, you're lucky you got out alive," Rye said in consolation.

"I guess," Jim agreed.

Rye suggested that they go to Tack, but Jim wouldn't accompany him and Rye wouldn't leave him by himself just then. They watched the barn cave in, burn awhile with increased vigor, then begin to die down. The gutted

163

soddy was losing its glow. The smoke cleared gradually, then when they went down finally the ground was cool enough to cross.

With the smoke less, the lingering fire cast the whole yard into bright illumination. It did not seem likely that anybody had been left behind, but they looked around. Across the creek, beyond the trees where the gunmen had covered the soddy door, they found a dead plow horse, a straw pad cinched to it, its halter rope still tied to a bush.

"Looks like the critter was in your line of fire," Rye said. "And this is sure a nester plug."

"I never sent a shot that high, Rye."

"Then who killed?"

"They did. To make this look like nester work."

"That makes sense."

Behind a cottonwood across the creek, when day had broken, they found bloodstains.

"If they're more Gallant riffraff and you killed him," Rye reflected, "they might just bury him and forget it. Otherwise there'll be a doctor or coroner needed. It might pay us to inquire into that of Winthrop."

Jim nodded. "I've got to go in to the inquest this morning. I'll check with him."

"I'm glad you don't need him, but you're sure a sight. You come down to Tack with me, Jim. You can't stay here."

Jim's face hardened. "Nobody's running me off my ranch, Rye. I'm staying here. I've still got the homestead, the cattle, and some horses, and I can borrow on them at the bank. I'll see about it today."

Feeling his heart warm, Rye said, "I've got no business to say this, Jim, since it's your own affair and she's made up her mind. But you hadn't ought to rebuild your headquarters here. Nora hadn't ought to be moving to Crown. With Bill gone, you ought to live on Tack with her and run both spreads as one. Martha says that; it was what Bill really wanted."

"What ought to be isn't what will," Jim answered. "You get on now. Martha must be worried about you."

"She don't even know I'm here. I was going home by myself when I seen the fire."

"Before you go will you loan me a horse while I round in mine? I expect they hit for the bench."

"I'll fetch them in for you," Rye said. He knew Jim needed to be left alone there with his loss, and without waiting for objections he turned and started for the bluff where he had left his horse.

He found Jim's horses grazing on the bench as serenely as if they had undergone no ordeal in the night. He brought them back, helped Jim repair the break in the fence. The barn that had formed one corner of the pasture was gone but, since the ruins still smoldered, would hold them in.

Rye pulled the saddle off his own horse, tossed the blanket over the fence. "You'll need these," he said. "I'll borrow another rig from Nora. You going to take a horse to Prairie to pack back grub and stuff to camp with?"

Jim nodded. Rye saw the fierce will in his eyes, knew that for all they had done to Jim they hadn't knocked him off his feet."

"And thanks, Rye," Jim said before Rye left.

"What for?"

"For coming in to get me. Not every man would have."

Rye only snorted and rode out.

He was beat up himself by then and so was his horse,

165

so they traveled at an easy jog. As he came down from the bench into the narrows he saw that the fire had burned itself out. For a moment he stopped the horse and looked back upon a scene of utter desolation where the day before had stood the finest crop of irrigated hay in Western Nebraska, the work of its strongest man. Alone now, he gave way to his private anguish, his eyes grew moist. It was partly for the breed that was vanishing, men like Charlie Vassey and Bill and maybe, at one time, himself, men of whom Jim so strongly reminded him, of which he was the last.

Martha apparently had been cooking breakfast at Tack—she'd be in the kitchen anyplace where there was one—for she saw Rye coming in bareback and rushed out into the yard. Not until he saw the expression on her face did he realize how the embers had eaten holes in his shirt and hat, the smoke blackened his features.

"Not a fire!" she cried. "Rye, what was it—the house?"

"Not ours," he said wearily as he slid off the horse. "Jim's buildings and hay are gone."

"No!" she protested. "How did it start?"

"Not by accident," Rye said bitterly.

Apparently Nora had been awake and listening. She came running out of the house, buttoning a wrapper over her nightgown, her feet bare, her loose hair jouncing.

"Did you say Jim's place?" she cried.

"Everything's gone but Jim," Rye told her. All at once he was enormously angry with this blind girl. He explained how he had noticed the fire, what he had found in the sink, told them of Jim's refusal to leave his ranch for anything or anybody this side of hell. Glaring, he said, "Nora, you're a plague-taken fool. I left the one

166

real man in the country down down there figuring out how to start over again."

She knew what he meant, he expected her to flare up, but instead she broke gaze and looked at the ground. Then, very quietly, "I know it, Rye."

"Then, by God, why're you marrying Peyt?"

She let a naked feeling show, one he had never seen in her before, a trapped look. "You don't understand. Peyt's always needed me. He can't get along without me. I promised him long ago that I'd marry him when we grew up. It's become a part of him. I can't break that promise or ask him to release me."

"Bill's gone," Rye returned, "and I'm the closest thing to a father you've got left. You've raised your son. He's a man now—cut him loose, make him stand on his own feet, wean him."

"I can't desert him."

"Do you love Jim?"

Instead of answering she turned and fled into the house.

"Maybe I oughtn't to have talked that way," Rye muttered.

"I'm glad you did," Martha said. "She does love Jim. When she heard what had happened to him she couldn't hide it. But you haven't changed her mind. Nothing will. You see, to a mother a son is never really grown-up."

CHAPTER 18

RODNEY GALLANT WAS AWAITING THE NOON HOUR, when the ultimatum he had given Peyton would expire. He had no doubt of its success. Peyt was brash, deadly,

167

but he also had a shrewd mind. Had he already been married to the Trevers girl, surer of his hold on her, it might make a difference. Now, when his first instinctive rebellion had died, he would reconsider. If he failed to do so, Gallant had a resort—his clerks, who had served his purposes admirably before. Peyt would change his tune if he was given to understand they had overheard the conversation the day Peyt so thinly, enticingly suggested the murder of Bill Trevers. The threat to reveal as much to the sheriff as a lead to the old man's death, with Peyt a direct suspect, would quickly bring the wily lad to time.

Meanwhile there was Carlin to be dealt with, and Gallant thought that would be accomplished at the inquest at ten o'clock. All yesterday, and again coming to the office that morning, he had been conscious of the natural tension in the town. The water that could make or break Prairie and the settlers about it was an obsessive matter, it worked on their nerves and created a strong antipathy toward any obstructive lake rancher. Carlin's wild, apparently senseless actions in killing the two rustlers on Prairie's own streets had inflamed this hostility as if the two mysterious figures had been bona fide settlers themselves.

Knowing it would work on Peyt, adding cogency in his mind, Gallant had encouraged this reckless resentment in the town, from which the coroner's jury— and later a grand jury—would have to be empaneled. As a surprise, he had two men ready to alibi the dead men for the hours in which Carlin insisted they had been on Tack range. After that bombshell there was no question what would happen to Jim Carlin, and this power in the settlers' own hands would convince Peyt he had better come to time.

Gallant kept looking at his watch, the hours dragging, and it still lacked thirty minutes until the inquest was to begin at the funeral parlor. To allow himself time to investigate, Sheriff Landorf had scheduled a single session to deal with all three deaths since Carlin claimed they were all of a piece. That would bring most of the lake ranchers to town, particularly Carlin and Trevers' daughter—who had been the last to see her father alive—and if for no other reason Peyt would naturally come in to comfort and support his fiancée through the ordeal.

Every so often Gallant would walk to the window and look out upon the street. He was already aware that a large number of settlers had come in from the back country, and this time he saw Carlin riding alone along the street. Gallant stared with bulging eyes, for the man wore neither a shirt nor a hat, and the hair seemed gone from his head. Stunned, at a panicky loss as to what had happened to him, Gallant felt his heart begin to speed up its beat. The man was so unpredictable, then so devastating when he took action, that anybody in his right senses would step wide of him if possible. Carlin rode on up the street, was lost from sight, and this fact alone increased Gallant's uneasiness.

He comforted himself with the thought that the next few hours would change matters; Carlin was certain to be bound over to the grand jury, it was doubtful that he could post bail, and that cleared the way for the final actions necessary to secure access to Silver Lake so that the contractor—for whom Gallant had wired the day before—could set at once to work. The upshot of it all would be the release of the funds Gallant could then draw from the bank, without which he would shortly be bankrupt.

Jim Carlin was glad to see that Prairie's bank was already open for business. He had been aware all along the street of the attention he drew, of the fact that, though there was curiosity as to his weird, half-naked appearance, a deep hostility was the main cause of the staring. Even as he tied his horse two burly young settlers halted, after swaggering past, and looked back at him truculently, as if tempted to turn back. Then, because of the gun on his hip, something in his eyes, they went on. Jim crossed to the bank door and entered.

Once, when this institution had been in Moccasin, it had been called the Drovers and Grangers Bank. When it left the dying town, the prefix had been changed tactfully to Grangers and Grazers. Jim had a little money there, he knew Orville Lee, the manager. When he saw Lee through the open door of a side office he walked in uninvited.

A short, thin man with a shoe-dauber mustache, Lee looked up in surprised irritation. Something in the black eyes he saw under the singed eyebrows made him uneasy, and he tried to laugh.

"Well, Jim, did you lose your shirt in a poker game?"

"I was burned out last night," Jim said. "I want to borrow money, but that's only part of what I come in for. You work both sides of the street, but you're a sound man, Lee. So are some of the others with money invested here. Why aren't you handling the water question instead of leaving it to Gallant? You could get farther and be surer of where you're going."

There was a sharpening of the native shrewdness in Lee's eyes. "What do you mean, get farther?"

"The thing has developed so far we've got to come to terms with the settlers. The movement Gallant started

170

has got too big. There's too many people on his tract that will be ruined if we don't help them. Just the same, we've got a right to our range."

"I've never thought otherwise," Lee agreed.

"Then put your bank behind a water company. Bring in some of the others who want to see this town stay alive. Give us an ironclad agreement to draw only so much water from Silver every year. Give us the right to cancel the contract if there's any more effort to invade our range. If you'll do that, I think I can get the cattle outfits to go along with it."

"Even Crown?" Lee asked in astonishment.

"I think even Crown," Jim said grimly.

"But how about Gallant?"

"If you take the play away from him, what can he do to stop it?"

Lee rose from his desk and took a few restless paces, staring at the floor. He nodded. "That's all right, Jim, but you might not be around long enough to throw your weight behind it."

"I'll take my chances."

"But this bank can't take chances like that. Gallant's a powerful man."

"You sound like a fool," Jim said hotly. "The cattle trade can still be important to you if you let it. Irrigation's here to stay. Every outfit on the lake could raise hay. This thing might be worked out to the benefit of everybody concerned. They'd need loans from you— I need one right now—and particularly Ellen Vassey. She's got to have medical treatment, which I'd like for her to get without having to sell the, Five to Crown. With your help, I'd see the Five raises enough hay to do that."

"You sound confident of coming clear of those

killings."

"I've done nothing wrong."

"But can you prove it?"

"No," Jim said. "Are you turning me down?"

"I've got to," Lee said with some regret, "until we know how you're going to make out."

As he left, Jim cashed a check, then went to a general store. There he bought a hat, shirt, and pants, and went into the back room to change. It was then nearly time for the inquest to start, and he went to the funeral parlor, only to find it locked up. Puzzled, he went to the Granger Hotel, where Bob Landorf, the sheriff, was putting up. He found Nora seated on the porch, Rye beside her, and was surprised that Peyt was not with her. There was a look of strain on her face, probably because this duty was a hard one for her.

Touching his new hat to her, Jim looked at Rye and said, "Where's the inquest?"

"Can't start yet," Rye said. "The clerk inside says the doctor was called out of town last night, and the sheriff went with him. They ain't back yet." His eyes held Jim's; they both would be interested to learn where the two men had gone. Then the old man added, "This is sure a steamed-up town. Even Nora's been getting dirty looks when the clodhoppers go by."

"As if," Nora said bitterly, "I had no right to be resentful myself."

"Do yourself any good at the bank?" Rye asked Jim with an old friend's license.

Jim shook his head. "Lee won't talk till I've cleared myself."

"I might as well be honest, Jim. I don't think too much of your chances."

Jim was surprised at the worry Nora put in the quick

172

look she gave Rye. It was nerves, probably. Disaster had piled on disaster until she expected nothing good at all any more. He wished he could comfort her but knew in his heart he might have trouble coming clear of the law. There weren't enough cattlemen any more, the nesters ruled the country, the juries, the county governments, the state.

Rye had turned his head, was staring down toward the west end of town. Glancing that way, Jim saw a group of riders appear at the end of the street, a buggy coming behind them. This aroused no excitement in him until, a minute or so later, he saw that the mounted men were Tex Rinehart and three other Crown punchers. Dr. Winthrop drove the following buggy and beside him in the seat was Bob Landorf. The sheriff had a rifle across his lap.

"What the hell?" Rye gasped, and Nora made a small, bewildered cry.

They all rushed down to the edge of the sidewalk. Landorf barked an order to the men ahead, and they pulled down sullenly.

"What you got there, Bob?" Rye asked urgently.

"The men," Landorf said grimly, "who burned Jim out last night."

"How do you know about that? He ain't even seen you since."

The sheriff eyed Nora hesitantly, then his face set. "You've got to hear, anyhow. I found out at Crown. Peyt Peyton's dead."

At Nora's sharp gasp Jim placed a hand on her arm. He saw the blood leave her face, her eyes closed, and she swayed. He put his arm quickly about her shoulders and pulled her against him. It passed, and her eyes opened again.

Quietly she said, "I want to hear it all."

173

"It's best, ma'am," Landorf said gently. "Rinehart come for Doc last night. Said Peyt had shot himself accidentally. A gunshot wound at a time like this is serious, and Doc come to me before he went out. I went with him. Peyt was gone when we got there. Rinehart said he dropped his pistol, it went off and drilled him. There was one thing wrong with that—the slug come out lower than it went in, or nearly come out. It was lodged against the spine, and when Doc dug it out it was a rifle bullet."

"Ah," Rye said, and Jim's eyes narrowed.

"Rinehart," Landorf resumed, "had tangled his rope so bad he got anxious to tell the truth. Said Peyt took them on a raid against Carlin last night, that it was go or lose their jobs, if you want to believe that. Peyt was hit, and it was all they could do to get him home alive. Peyt ordered him to tell the story about the accident. Said Peyt once admitted intending to take all the country around the lake, that there was a tie-in with Gallant, too. So I brought 'em in—material witnesses as well as for destroying property and malicious assault. They all preferred that to being charged with killing Peyt and trying to cover it up with that lie."

"How about the inquest?" Rye asked.

"They're bringing Peyt in. We'll thresh the whole thing out at once. But I'm a lot less worried about you than I was, Jim." Landorf spoke another gruff order and his prisoners moved on, the buggy following.

Jim looked down at Nora's stricken face and said, "I'm sorry."

"It wasn't your fault," Rye said bitterly. "You didn't even know who was out there."

"No, Jim," Nora agreed. "You had to do it. I'm glad it was him—not you."

174

Gallant's confidence received a shaking when he saw Nora Trevers ride into town with old Rye Jones. The thought crossed his mind that Peyt meant to defy him, was staying away. Then, a little later, when he saw the sheriff come in with four Crown riders, the confidence broke completely and he knew that something had gone perilously wrong. He watched the group stop before the Granger but from his position could not see who was on the sidewalk. He took a restless turn around the floor, stunned, worried.

He had to know what had happened so, clapping his hat on his head, he walked out to the hallway, then descended the stairs. At the door he pulled a cigar from his pocket and lighted it, covertly glancing along the street, seeing Trevers' girl there on the walk before the hotel with Carlin and Jones. He felt sweat run down his neck, his fingers trembled so he could barely hold the flame to the tip of the cigar. Some settlers had stopped behind the group, were listening. Presently the sheriff's party came on, and as it passed it seemed to Gallant that Landorf stared at him with a hard intentness. Gallant managed to tip a casual nod, which Landorf failed to return. There was a brittle anger on Dr. Winthrop's face. The four men who, from the rifle, were obviously prisoners only stared dully ahead.

Gallant remained where he was until the settlers came up, four men who had bought what they expected to become farms on the tract. They looked disturbed, and he saw they intended to stop, their eyes hardening notably.

"What's the excitement?" he managed to ask.

"Peyton's dead. What's that going to do to the canal?"

175

The feigned aplomb was gone from Gallant, he dropped his cigar. "Peyton—dead?" he gasped.

"That's what the sheriff said. Tried to raid somebody's ranch last night and got shot. Who owns Crown now, Gallant? Who are you going to buy your right-of-way from?"

Gallant could only turn and hurry up the stairs, his pulse crashing in his ears. He could have answered the settler's question. Peyt had no heirs, Crown would be tied up through all the long, slow processes of law that Gallant had tried to avoid. He reached his desk and dropped into the chair. He knew already that he was finished. The anger he had helped engender in Prairie would in another hour be turned on him. In the very least they would demand their money back, they might go to greater extremes.

He had been in tight spots before, but never one like this. Yet the experience helped him accept the fact of his ruin, to plan what to do to save himself as much as he could. He had practically no money left, now that the ditch question might not be settled for a year or more, his creditors would bring him down. Already the contractor would be shipping his machinery, preparing to hire and ship out men. He would demand enormous damages when the work could not be started.

Slowly Gallant's anger focused on Jim Carlin, who, one way or another, had frustrated him at every turn. He yearned to even the score but knew that he dared not press at the inquest. The shady settlers who had agreed to help him would back out now that it was evident they were themselves in trouble. Carlin would come free, and, besides, there was no telling what Peyt might have divulged before he died. Gallant knew he had to take the chicken feed in the safe and leave the country as swiftly as he could.

Opening his desk, he got his gun and slipped it into his pocket. He took the currency out of the safe and stuffed it in another pocket. He still had his hat on and, resolved, he went out through the general office, saying to his clerks, "I'll be at the inquest if you need me," sounding so casual about it he surprised himself. He took the back stairway, reached the alley, and crossed over to the rear door of the hotel. A moment later he was in his quarters there, intending only to pick up his most valuable possessions and make his definite plan.

Looking at his watch, he saw that the westbound was due in less than an hour. He dared not board it here, but it would stop for water at Cheyenne Well, some five miles up the track. As far as he knew, the inquest would soon be held, now that the sheriff and coroner were back. While it riveted attention, he would make his way to the livery. He had been generous with the hostler, who wouldn't try to trick and stop him. On a good horse he would have a fair chance of getting aboard the train at the tank stop, if that failed, he would ride on somewhere, anywhere to get away from this town.

He got what he wanted, some money he had in the room, some papers that were important to him. That was all, since he didn't want to be encumbered. Parting the curtains a little, he looked out to see men hurrying along the street, all going in the same direction. Presently they thinned out, then nobody was going past. Gallant's confidence came up. He walked out into the hallway and through the lobby, nodding cheerfully to the man on the desk. He hesitated in the street doorway long enough to make sure there was no one on the porch, that Carlin and his friends had moved on. Gallant slid his hand into his pocket, gripped the gun.

As he came out he saw the settlers who had been

hurrying past a while ago congregated before the bank. His nerves tightened when he realized they were there either to demand the money they had in escrow or because his office was upstairs. He had no time to waste, so he moved boldly onto the street and started across. He reached the far walk, meaning to go on and make his way along a side street to the livery barn. But a voice rang out behind him.

"Gallant—citizen's arrest—for murder!"

Gallant whirled in horror at the familiarity of that voice, those words. Carlin was coming toward him, apparently had been waiting around the corner of the hotel, keeping an eye on its front and rear. All the rage he had ever felt against the man swirled up in Gallant. His mind's eye saw Rankin in this same situation, and reflexively he did what Rankin had tried. The gun in his pocket roared and missed, then Carlin was drawing as Gallant fired desperately again.

Carlin's gun answered, and as Gallant fell he had the old illusion of the town he had created not being there at all, then suddenly he was himself still and empty in that emptiness.

We hope that you enjoyed reading this
Sagebrush Large Print Western.
If you would like to read more Sagebrush titles,
ask your librarian or contact the Publishers:

United States and Canada

Thomas T. Beeler, *Publisher*
Post Office Box 659
Hampton Falls, New Hampshire 03844-0659
(800) 251-8726

United Kingdom, Eire, and
the Republic of South Africa

Isis Publishing Ltd
7 Centremead
Osney Mead
Oxford OX2 0ES England
(01865) 250333

Australia and New Zealand

Australian Large Print Audio & Video P/L
17 Mohr Street
Tullamarine, Victoria, 3043, Australia
1 800 335 364